Fragrance
of
Beauty

"This mini-beauty course of ABC requirements for enhancing outward beauty is very basic, but it might mean the difference between confirming and denying the faith that is within you.

"It would be wonderful if we could stand at a distance and see ourselves as God and men see us. Maybe we would immediately be able to properly evaluate our looks.

"But all we really have is God's mirror (His Word) for our faith and our dressing room mirror for our face. Let's use them both enthusiastically to be the beautiful women of faith and face God intended."

—Joyce Landorf Heatherley

While this book is designed for reading enjoyment and individual instruction, it is intended also for group study. A leader's guide is available from your local bookstore or from the publisher.

Fragrance of Beauty

JOYCE
LANDORF HEATHERLEY

BALCONY PUBLISHING

AUSTIN, TEXAS 78734

Fragrance of Beauty Copyright 1990 Joyce V. Heatherley. Published by Balcony Publishing Company, Austin, Texas.
Originally copyrighted 1973 Victor Books, titled *The Fragrance of Beauty*.

Library of Congress Catalog Card Number 90-92683
ISBN Number 929488-16-4

Printed in the United States of America

To: A Woman
Who gave herself totally to Christ,
Who was granted freedom by God's forgiveness,
Who has dropped her insecurities, hang-ups, and fears
    at the Cross,
    and
Who now walks with her head held high,
    in the sunshine of God's love
    and is surrounded by the
    incredible fragrance of His beauty:
        Clare Bauer

To: These Women,

Who beautifully typed rough drafts,
Who diligently added commas and parentheses,
Who faithfully corrected my spelling,
Who lovingly typed the completed manuscript, and
Who continually encouraged me:
      Brenda Arnold
      Adeline Griffith
      Wendy Justice
      Pamela McGraw
      Pris Norton
      Sheila Rapp

CONTENTS

Introduction

When our company, Balcony Publishing, began receiving requests for us to put *Fragrance of Beauty* back into print, I should have guessed that the day was not too far off when my husband and publisher, Francis, would announce, "Oh, about revising *Fragrance* . . . I think it is time . . . "

So, here I sit rereading a book I wrote back, way back, in 1973, trying to strategize how I'll handle rewrites, updates, and plain old out-takes. I'm beginning to get the strong impression that while some things seem to remain forever and constant, many other things flutter in the continual winds of change. I'm not saying that the true essence or fragrance of beauty has changed or lessened, but we women, well, we seem to do nothing but change! In some ways our changes as women are as transforming as the ancient metamorphosis from the fuzzy caterpillar to the splendid butterfly. Other changes make me uncomfortable and I struggle with my own "image" within and without. However, I'm still in love with the unique fragrance of beauty as I see it reflected in the faces and lives of the women I meet on a daily basis.

As I began to reread and tackle this update, two names rose out of the first pages and they warmed my heart with memories—scented by roses and lilies of the valley. I began

Fragrance Of Beauty with a dedication to the classic beauty, Clare Bauer. Then in Chapter One, I described a conversation about beauty with another beautiful woman, Perky Brandt.

Before my first book was published in 1968, I met both of these women, and they were destined to become very dear to me. Over night, it seemed, we became dear and personal friends. As I reviewed our friendship, what struck me as being quite wonderful was that since our friendships blossomed, both women have weathered remarkably the sometimes-excruciating twists, tests, and turns of events for all these years (nearly thirty now). And, they have *remained* my treasured friends. How good it feels that neither of them has, at any time, decided to check out of the relationship temporarily or permanently. Nor did they at any time abandon me or admonish me to "get my act together," or to "change my attitudes or choices." It blesses my socks off that neither one of them said, "Joyce, you know we should avoid even the 'appearance of evil', so I'll be praying for you privately, but I can't be seen publicly with you." No. Not at all! Steadfastly they've maintained and continued to nurture and nourish our history   together—no matter where we lived or how many times a year we were actually together. They've been true friends through the good, the glorious, and the ghastly times.

They are real "balcony people" to me, but perhaps the factor that is most remarkable to me is that while we all have celebrated our fiftieth birthdays, Clare and Perky are simply shimmering and deliciously fragrant with inner and outer beauty. When I'm with either one of them, I'm always a bit taken aback at how the aging process has only made them lovelier. It is no mystery that people of all ages seek them out and just want to be in their presence.

In taking a fresh look at Clare and Perky today, after all these years, I sensed that these two delightful friends add validity to the concepts of this writing. So, I'm glad that this book is to be reissued, because it gives me a chance to introduce the reality of God's fragrance in our lives to a new generation or two.

I still believe in the wonder of God's fragrance in our lives, and I still believe in the principles of these concepts as we allow the beauty of Christ to develop and enhance our daily living, and I still cherish the truth that women like Clare and Perky make me proud to be a Christian woman. They also make me joyously aware of all my sisters in the Body, the Church, and the community who are exquisite proof of the ageless, fadeless, effervescent glowing scent of beauty! As the old chorus sings, "Let the beauty of Jesus be seen in ... "

So be it, Lord. So be it!

Joyce Landorf Heatherley

ONE

Man Certainly Does Look on the Outside!

It all started with my meeting Perky Brandt, the pastor's wife, on the night of their Mother and Daughter Banquet at her church. It was only minutes after Perky and I were introduced and seated at the head table before we began to compare childhoods and the church women stereotypes we both knew. We found that we had so much in common as we traded stories about our church-related childhoods. It was amazing and amusing. In general, you could say we giggled our way through that whole dinner. Not once did we act dignified—like a pastor's wife or a banquet speaker should have. We were more comparable to two junior high school girls, acting silly and speaking a foreign language only we could understand.

Several months after our meeting, we were having a phone conversation when my new friend Perky grew serious. As a minister's wife, she was expressing some growing concerns about the women in their congregation. She talked not only of women's physical looks, but of their attitudes and needs as well.

"The women come in all shapes, sizes, and ages, and from different backgrounds, but somehow they all look alike." Perky commented and then added, "I think it has something to do with inner beauty (or their lack thereof), but whatever is going on *inside* seems to affect their outer looks too."

Perky's voice took on a mischievous tone, so I was alerted to the fact that she was about to make a "we" statement that would draft me into an "I" response. Sure enough.

"Do you suppose, as Christian women, we (there it was) need some kind of a charm course or self-improvement workshop?"

My immediate reaction was a quick no. I reasoned that Christian women didn't need *any* course, books, or lessons on beauty. After all, when a woman truly accepts Christ, the Creator of all beauty, as her Savior, isn't she as radiant as a bride? Isn't she beautiful, just knowing she is loved and allowing the Lord Himself to shine through her? Of course she is!

But my next thought was, "Or is she?"

All those speaking and singing engagements of mine provided the perfect opportunity for taking a good look at Christian women. But before I go on, I must make one thing clear. I deplore—especially in our American culture—the continual, incessant worship of beauty and youth. All you need is one flaw, one physical or one emotional defect, and you cannot qualify for the beautiful-people set. Unfortunately, "rich and thin is in!"

There is not a line in this writing intended to give support to an already over-worshiped beauty cult. Rather, I pray that this book will help us all to take a good look at the women in our own mirrors. Then, perhaps we can sanely evaluate all our vital statistics in their proper relationship to our lives and discover ways to minimize our flaws and maximize our strengths.

When I began to take a purely academic look at my audiences, at the women in my own church, and yes, especially at myself, I did see a need.

Later in this book I want to develop some of the hows and whys of inner beauty, but first, let me tell you what I saw on the *outside* of Christian women.

I started with teen-age girls. I lived with one fantastic specimen—my daughter Laurie—and true to form for most teen-agers, she almost died if she didn't look *exactly* like everyone else at school. Don't frown, Mother. Remember that every generation speaks its own language, hears its own music, and claims its own trends. And the kids of each generation wear their own get-ups. There were the sloppy Joe sweaters of the forties, the sweater sets of the fifties, the jeans of the sixties, the layered look of the seventies, and the tattered-and-torn look of the eighties. Peer pressure aside, when I looked at teen-agers, I saw a need to develop positive feelings of self-worth far more than I did to develop skills for facial makeup, because the roller-coaster emotions of the teen years can be pretty painful. At this point, however, I was not looking inwardly—just concentrating on the outward impressions. While most teen-aged girls had little or no idea what makeup was best for their facial shape or coloring, observation told me that they readily accepted the concept of *doing something* about their physical appearance. In fact, face makeup and hair were uppermost in their minds and conversations.

Then my eye fell on other teen-aged girls who were so turned off by the beauty-worship rituals of our society that they went as far as they could go in the opposite direction. Their goal was to be as plain, as ugly, and as unattractive as possible. In view of society's continual stress on the need to be beautiful, I understood their rebellion, though I can't say I thought it was very attractive.

The next age group I studied was the twenty-five to thirty-five-year-old women. They were very divided in looks. Most of these women were mothers of babies and/ or very young children. About half of this group were sparkling and vivacious; they seemed to have left their ugly, awkward stages completely behind. Their faces were alive with individualized beauty. Their clothing, makeup, and poise seemed very tasteful. I wondered a bit about their secret ways of staying so lovely.

The other half were a different story. Married or single, they seemed to lack the luster and glow of their own peer group. It seemed to me that their general attitude toward clothes, makeup, and poise was one of apathy or maybe just plain carelessness. Fatigue, depression, and an odious disrespect for their own minds and bodies seemed to be written across their lives. It showed in their posture and the way they walked. I watched one young mother as she brought a coldness into the atmosphere of the room and then slumped heavily down into her chair. She presented a fairly accurate picture of the whole ambiance of her life. But I also saw this same attitude reflected in the face of a single woman and a single mother. Their faces had hardened into icy masks and they broke my heart with the despair and despondency I saw.

The thirty-five to fifty-year-olds were the most interesting. At this age, when I would have thought we would have matured out of earlier inferiority complexes, many of us (me included) seem to be dragged down by them. Our children were older and less demanding, so I assumed that fatigue would not be such a problem. Yet, loneliness and boredom showed on the faces of this group, as well as on mine. Ironically, at this time of life, when I could afford cosmetics, haircuts, and at least occasional visits to the hairdresser, my looks and those of my peers seemed to need the most help. Skin and hair problems were quite evident. And worse, the flabbiness and lumpiness of our figures indicated that we had neglected one of the best techniques of preventive medicine: *exercise*.

I had long carried a mental image of the typical Christian woman as one who might be plain-featured, but one who, because of Christ's inner glow radiating from her heart to her face, is beautiful in her own special way. But where were these beautiful-in-Christ women I was hoping to find? Why, in my quest, had I not seen many such beautiful women? Had it always been like this?

I searched my memory, back to when I was ten years old. The women of our church were instantly recognizable then. I wish I could say they were recognizable because of love, joy, and the beauty of Christ, but that was simply not true in most cases.

If three pagan women and one Christian woman were waiting for a bus at the corner, you could instantly tell which one was the Christian. She was always the least attractive one. *Saturday Nite Live's* characterization of the Church Lady—"Isn't that special?" is unfortunately quite an accurate picture of the Christian women in my childhood.

The Christian woman of that day prided herself on the alleged fact that she wore no makeup. I say "alleged" because she usually broke form to apply a layer of very white powder. Her hair was rarely cut or permed, and many times it was pulled tightly back into a small bun. Sometimes it was just left hanging and bobby pinned on the sides. Her dress was usually a somber, dreary navy or black number in a "sensible" style of some year long past.

But while the Christian woman looked like a misfit at the bus stop, in church circles it was a different story. She was considered "very spiritual." (I used to think, "Yes, quite unattractive but definitely spiritual".)

For a time, my own mother was caught in this trap and felt that she too had to *look* spiritual in order to *be* spiritual. I guess nobody had come up with the theory that if you *are* spiritual, you will *look* spiritual. Most Christian women continued to put the cart before the horse. My mother did understand how important inner enthusiasm is to one's own beauty; and, in that sense, she was gorgeous!

But once in a while Mother "copped out" and rebelled against the drab bleak looks of her day. I remember in particular a navy blue dress that was completely embroidered with tiny red and yellow flowers and bright kelly green leaves. I loved the way she looked in it. The ladies in my father's church, however, had a far different reaction. They felt the dress had "too much color . . . especially red" and that when Pastor's wife wore it she lost a great deal of her spiritual depth. Then, without much grace, the women made the whole thing a matter of discussion and prayer at the next Ladies' Missionary Society meeting. Much to my delight, Mother wore it anyway the following Sunday. Actually, she continued to wear it rather gleefully until finally the ladies began questioning my *father's* spirituality. After that, the dress disappeared into a chest, and some months later it was given to me to use as a "play dress-up" dress. A photograph I have on my shelf today shows my parents and me at that time . . . my mother is wearing *that* dress. Her spirit and enthusiasm for life still makes me smile!

Anyway, in those days it was safe to assume that most Christian women were not glowingly beautiful. I feel much of that was changed by a very imaginative woman who came along in the thirties—Aimee Semple McPherson, a woman preacher in Los Angeles, California.

She exploded on the colorless, dull church scene, as we knew it, with a burst of flamboyance that astounded everyone. Her outrageous behavior reached from California to the little town in Ontario, Canada, where I lived, and where Christians gossiped about her. My *how* they endlessly gossiped and talked about her! First it was rumored, and then positively reported, "Aimee wore makeup to church." Whether you agreed with her theology or not, you had to admit she could sing and preach, and furthermore she looked extremely beautiful while doing it. Such a phenomenon! We were all stunned in our little Canadian town, and you should have heard the talk and the prayer time at the Ladies' Missionary Meeting each week.

When Aimee preached in elegant evening gowns, we were all properly stunned (again). When she took the hottest fashion garments of the day—capes—and dressed her choir and usherettes in them, most of us felt that was the last straw of worldliness. But Aimee went on and on. Her makeup and clothing were very tame by today's standards, but back then, my ... the controversy she caused! Men professed to be shocked and women silently ate their little hearts out.

Evidently Aimee was also deeply concerned about the dreary, ugly church auditoriums of those days, for she helped design one of the most beautiful sanctuaries anyone had seen, even in the "free-wheeling" West. (It was shockingly similar to a theater and quite a departure for church architecture.)

Beauty, gorgeous beauty, came to church, and Aimee Semple McPherson was certainly responsible for that trend. Out went the drab platforms of the day and in came a beautifully designed stage, which became the scene for illustrated sermons, and it was one of the first to have a full orchestra and a complete band. Christian musicals, operas, and dramas were also presented on that stage. Even the ordinary straight-across-the-back balcony didn't stay in its place, but gloriously curved around and down to the front of the sanctuary. Aimee's church was a design that ended up being copied over and over again. It seemed to me that Aimee was making far more than a dramatic statement on church architecture. I could almost hear her pioneering a message to Christian women. "Women, you don't have to be ugly and plain to prove how spiritual you are. Actually, you have absolutely the biggest potential of all women to be creatively and positively beautiful—inwardly *and outwardly!*"

In Christian circles today, the percentage of lovely, attractive, beautifully groomed women has certainly increased from those days in the thirties. There is a definite decline in the number of hold-outs trying to "look spiritual," and for this I'm grateful. But what disturbed my friend Perky, and subsequently aroused me, was the large segment of Christian women who, while they were dressed neatly and modestly, still had the drab, worn-out-bathrobe look. They could have been vastly more attractive in other areas—hair, skin, figure, posture, and poise—but many were not doing anything about their uniqueness or their own special qualities, and I saw so much *unused potential.*

The founder and director of one of the first Christian charm and modeling schools I knew of, said, "So many times the average Christian woman of today wants to be so 'spiritual' that she has lost her prettiness, her natural flair for beauty. In fact, she is *so* basic she's boring."

I personally wish with all my heart that this statement were not accurate, but I'm afraid it is. The key words in it are "lost . . . her natural flair for beauty" and "she is . . . boring."

After I had shared the results of my "research" about the feminine beauty scene with Perky, we outlined a program for women of her church called GLO. It called for three morning sessions starting at 9:00 A.M. with coffee and danish. Classes ran from 9:30 until noon. The women would bring sack lunches and eat together. Also, a nursery would be provided.

The first session was called *Glamour*. I designed a very general, basic course on makeup, skin care, and hair treatment and talked about *outward* beauty.

The next session was called *Living*. For this session, I brought about twenty handmade items from my home. Some were simple, but all were very pretty, yet functional and practical. I made some things from ideas found in magazines; others I made after I'd taken a night course at the local high school. I talked about developing skills in homemaking and the value it adds to our own personal estimation of our self-worth. Part of this included a discussion about eating and dressing on a limited budget.

The third and last session was be called *Opportunity*. I outlined a process by which God can inwardly transform ugliness into His loveliness. I then described some of the destructive things that could rob any woman, Christian or not, of the priceless commodity called beauty.

At this point Perky told her church women about the proposed GLO series, but before she could even set a date to begin, she got the first negative feedback. It seemed that some of the older ladies, reverting to the days of "looking spiritual," felt that we must remember that man looks on the outside but God looks on the inside. They felt women should concern themselves only with *inner* beauty and not dwell on their *outer* appearances at all. "Really," they said, "wasn't 1 Peter 3:3 clear on that point when he wrote 'Whose adorning let it not be that outward adorning of plaiting the hair, and of wearing of gold, or of putting on of apparel?'" (KJV).

When I heard this, I had to smile, because that very week a bedraggled-looking, Christian woman who hadn't bothered to comb her hair, sat in my living room, and with a voice full of self-pity whined, "I just can't figure it out! I've been a faithful wife, a good cook, and a good mother to our children, but my husband never looks at me any more; he never says 'I love you' and never gives me a compliment. I just don't understand it!"

I thought, "You're wrong about your husband never looking at you. Actually, your husband probably *has* looked at you but what he saw when he caught a glimpse of your hairdo and figure made him feel that he didn't want to look any farther. Your outward appearance turned him off and it was all he saw. The way you looked made him feel he didn't have any incentive to express his love."

While it's true that God beholds our inner beauty, inner motives, inner thoughts and dreams, we should remember that mankind has *nowhere else to look* but on the outward appearance!

When a man sees a woman, he looks first at her physical qualifications. It's sort of a built-in natural trait with him. He'll look at her face and figure, and not even necessarily in that order. But if a woman has a marvelous inner fragrance of beauty that is of God, then it's just possible that the man may see the shining reflection of God. The outer and inner looks can blend into one picture and when it does a beautiful woman emerges. That kind of woman is warm, giving, alert, fun to be with, loving, and yes, spiritual, but she also has an earthly sexiness that is uncommonly beautiful. Even though he may not say it, you know he's thinking "Wow!".

But what about Peter's warnings against outward adorning? As I read that third chapter, I believe the Apostle was warning us about getting carried away with the *pursuit* of beauty. He was urging us not to be *overly concerned* about what we wore or what our outer appearances looked like, and he was pointing out to us that our highest priority should be tending to developing our inner and spiritual qualities. The key words here are "overly concerned." I am confident that this is the emphasis that Peter meant to give—for if we carried out his words to their *literal* extent, those words would require that women go nude. "Whose adorning let it not be that of . . . putting on of apparel."

I can take Peter's gentle warning in the best of spirits because he really endears himself to me when, in that same chapter, he tells the *husbands* to be careful how they treat their wives, who are "partners in receiving God's blessings." What a news bulletin that must have been in that age of complete male dominance! Then he writes sternly, "And if you don't treat her as you should, your prayers will not get ready answers" (1 Peter 3:7).

But back to Perky's church. The need still existed; so after we'd examined these and other Scriptures on beauty, and after we had prayed and talked some more, we enthusiastically decided to go ahead with the GLO series, in spite of the negative feedback.

The success was marvelous, and even though this happened years ago, I'm still reminded of it periodically by someone who attended. Sometime after the series, as I was shopping in our local grocery store, a woman came up the aisle and chatted briefly with me. Since she really did look lovely, I told her so. She thanked me and then added, "You know, every time I get ready to go anywhere, I remember what you said in the GLO series about Christian women wearing those big pink hair curlers in public, so I stop and take special pains to see that my hair is combed and brushed." Then she added, "And I feel so special." She looked it, too.

I'm sure our husbands don't expect our figures and faces to rival those of some Hollywood movie star. But from talking to a great many men while researching this book, I found that they would like for us to do a bit more with the assets we already have. It seems men want women to look like *women*! The men who responded to my question, "What trait would you want to change in your wife?" seemed with one voice to say, "She should be more of a woman, inside and out." I'm not enough of a psychologist to know *exactly* what they meant, but I have a few ideas.

Peter warned women about being overly concerned with beauty that *depends* on jewelry, clothes, or hair arrangement, but he also said,"Be beautiful inside, in your hearts, with the lasting charm of a gentle and quiet spirit which is so precious to God" (1 Peter 3:4).

A gentle and quiet spirit is not only precious to God, but to others as well. Perhaps charm and beauty depend on a balance involving our not getting too wrapped up in the outward, yet not ignoring it either. It is striving for that incredible shining, inner beauty that truly "outglows" any other kind. *It is making the best of the original you that God designed and created.*

Once Margaret, my mother-in-law, and I had lunch in the elegant tea room of Bullock's Department Store. It turned out to be more fun than we guessed, because along with lunch we were treated to a fantastic fashion show. The clothes were gorgeous designer originals, and all of the women who modeled were rare examples of pure beauty. One model, however, outshone all of them. She had only to set one toe through the stage curtain and we found ourselves wildly applauding! She was so beautiful I felt that if she had come on stage in a burlap sack, we would have still thought her exquisite! She was a lovely montage of God's finest handiwork from her shining, vibrant-looking red hair, her peaches and cream complexion, her flawless figure, down to her long perfectly sculptured legs. She was the undisputed hit of the fashion show.

After lunch, my mother-in-law and I were still raving about her. Then as we continued to shop, we saw two of the models from the show standing at the end of a counter. It looked as if they were waiting for someone, and, it wasn't long until we saw who, because rushing across the store (leaving a trail of staring people behind her), came the gorgeous red-haired model.

Once again we were awestruck by the woman's incredible beauty, but only briefly, for even before she reached her friends, her mouth opened and out poured a barrage of the filthiest, most critical, and angriest language we'd ever heard. She was absolutely furious at the fashion coordinator, the clothes, the time limit, and a certain "blonde" whom she felt had tried to steal the show. While I was absorbed in all this, I suddenly realized that my eyes were doing strange things. The longer this beautiful woman talked and the longer I watched, the more she began to change right before my eyes.

To me it seemed the brilliant, dancing highlights in her red hair dulled considerably. Her eyelashes, once long black sweeps of beauty, grew shorter and became ugly stumps. On her skin, red blotches appeared and scars from a latent teen-age case of acne surfaced. Then her hips and thighs began to thicken and look like lumpy gravy. Her once-slim ankles looked exactly as mine had when I was nine months pregnant with Rick, Laurie and David and retaining all fluids.

In short, before my very eyes, the most beautifully endowed woman I'd ever seen turned disgustingly ugly. Her outward beauty was lost in the vile outpouring of her soul. I knew it was only a trick my eyes were playing on me, but it was quite effective.

Evidently we need to develop all areas of beauty—outer and inner. But what really is true beauty?

I believe the fragrance of true beauty begins inside of us and gradually seeps through our faces, our bodies, and our verbal expressions.

I also believe true beauty is latent, and lying dormant in all women. Some are blessed of God with both truly great outward and inward beauty. But most women I know have a certain *quality* of beauty rather than a whole suitcase of it. Truly wise is the woman who accurately perceives both her assets and her shortcomings and does the most with what she's got.

I believe, too, that true beauty must be more than skin deep. In a recent *People Magazine* (the summer 1990 edition that featured pictures of *The 50 Most Beautiful People in the World*), an oriental beauty cited was the Chinese actress, Vivian Wu. She was quoted as saying, "In China, being beautiful is more than on the face—you have to be kind and good to people." Also featured was another handsome Chinese actor, John Lone who said, "Thank you for saying I'm beautiful. On a superficial level, beauty has to do with proportions and harmony. It excites you and makes you more curious. But, it doesn't last. Real beauty has to do with the humanity in you and how you communicate beyond words."

I invite you, here and now, to take a good look into your mirror and an even closer look down into your soul. I also invite you to examine the claims of Christ, the Originator of all beauty, for without Him one hasn't a chance of remaining beautiful inside or out. Without Him, you could look like a beautiful model at Bullock's fashion show and still be ugly. With Him, you could have a very "plain Jane" face and yet display a deep and lasting beauty.

I'm writing this with the prayer that the fragrance of God's beauty will enfold and surround your entire being.

Being beautiful in Jesus very definitely involves both our inner soul's condition and our outer appearance. One confirms or denies the other. They are both important. Neither must be slighted.

While I'm sure the Apostle Paul was not considered a beauty expert in his day or ours either, nevertheless I think he has set down a statement about our lives as Christians that may be particularly applied to our beauty as women . . . more specifically to the *fragrance* of beauty about us.

"But thanks be to God! For through what Christ has done, He has triumphed over us so that now wherever we go, He uses us to tell others about the Lord and to spread the Gospel like a sweet perfume. As far as God is concerned, there is a sweet wholesome fragrance in our lives. It is the fragrance of Christ within us, an aroma to both the saved and the unsaved all around us"
(2 Corinthians 2:14,15).

It is true, as the next verse points out, that not everyone will appreciate our fragrant beauty, no matter how Christlike and outwardly attractive we may be. The very fragrance of our lives in Christ may be an offensive smell to some, because they don't want, or they can't acknowledge, the Christ in us.

In this sense, the familiar saying, "Beauty is in the eye of the beholder," finds its deepest and most profound validation. Even the altogether lovely Christ "hath no form nor comeliness and . . . no beauty that we should desire Him" to those people who love their sins (Isaiah 53:2, KJV).

In any case, we Christians are being constantly evaluated and watched. Our lives do speak out to others. The beauty of Christ ought to come forth continually, so let's examine our inner selves and our outer looks and determine exactly what fragrance fills the air around us.

"If a woman's soul is without cultivation, without taste, without refinement, without sweetness of a happy mind, not all the mysteries of art can ever make her face beautiful ... I find no art which can atone for an unpolished mind and an unlovely heart."[1]

---

[1] *The Arts and Secrets of Beauty* by Madame Lola Montez, 1853, Chelsea House Publishers, New York, NY, 1969.

TWO

Fear: A Roaring Lion

There are several inner conflicts that can plunder and rob a woman of her natural beauty. As Perky Brandt told me recently, "The two most negative emotions in our lives are those of fear and resentment." So let's look at one of these perpetrators of inner conflicts: FEAR.

A woman can be beautifully coiffured, expertly made up, and properly groomed; yet, if fear has vandalized the inner chambers of her soul, then her face, her walk, and her words will betray her. Almost nothing she can do disguises the disastrous results of fear.

In one of my mother's notebooks, I found these wonderfully descriptive lines:

Where Worry is a mouse,
    a small scampering thing with sharp tiny feet,
    that scurries over our souls—
Fear is a roaring lion,
    with huge paws, extended claws and teeth
    that slash us into strips.

I've seen and felt this lion at work—roaring, tearing, maiming, and paralyzing all movement—not only in my life but in the lives of many women. At one time or another, we are all the lion's victim.

A tense young woman nervously understates, "I'm afraid my marriage is over."

A bank teller honestly faces up to a reality of life when she whispers to me, "My only fear is the fear of death."

A distraught young wife, biting at the edge of what was once a long fingernail says, "My husband has been out of work for months; we may have to go into bankruptcy ... there is no financial security left any more and I'm afraid. I'm scared to death."

A woman, barely able to control her ravaged emotions, trembles as she blurts out, "My worst fears have come true. What I've suspected for years is now confirmed. My husband says he has never loved me, that he is gay ... a practicing homosexual ... and he is leaving me. What will I do? I'm so afraid."

A mother, admitting a fear that has become a reality for the first time, whispers, "My son is on drugs ... I am terrified for fear of what will happen to him."

A young bride thinks it is silly of her, yet she confesses, "Every time Ron is even a little late coming home from work, I just know he has been in an accident, is hurt, or worse ... is dead ... and I can't do anything but panic."

An older woman remembers her childhood and reminisces, "If I came home from school and nobody was there, I'd always be scared to death that the Lord had come back and I had been left behind. That was my biggest childhood fear."

A teen-age girl, twisting with the weight of an enormous guilt, stammers, "I'm going to have a baby ... and I'm scared to death to tell my Mom. She'll just freak out ... what am I going to do?"

A woman in her thirties confides to me that she was a victim of incest by her father. When I ask why she kept it a secret so long or why she didn't tell her mother, teacher, friend, or someone, she answers "I was afraid no one would believe me."

Another young woman, after years of trying to have a baby and making endless trips to the fertility doctors, hears her "biological clock" ticking and is full of fear as she sees her dream dying.

In my own life, the fear of failure on other issues still prowls about the edges of my subconscious mind.

These fears, including some of my own, have been expressed and brought out into the open where they could be examined. But for every shared fear, there are probably many unspoken fears, hidden fears, even unacknowledged fears, that lie just beneath the surface in many a woman's life.

When our emotions are controlled by our fears, we share the same look. The same panic and the same destruction is written across our faces and is reflected from our eyes. Fear *is* powerful. It is a panic in the blood, and it attacks our hearts.

Everyone of us can fall prey to the roaring lion of fear. Even David, the King of Israel, wrote, "My heart is in anguish within me. Stark fear overpowers me" (Psalm 55:4). Fear can and often does cause complete blockage to one's normal, rational thinking pattern, and it is an emotion that can paralyze all movement. David expertly diagnosed his problem when he wrote, "I am losing all hope; I am paralyzed with fear" (Psalm 143:4).

It is entirely possible to be a child of God (or even the King of Israel) and still experience the stark power of fear. I do not want to give the impression that as Christian women we will never have *any* fear. That's simply not true. We are all susceptible to the roaring lion of fear that would rip away at us. I know I certainly am. I'll tell you when a doctor says to me, "Joyce, I don't want to alarm you; however, we have found ... ," you know *I am alarmed* before he even finishes the sentence! That I am instantly struck with fear is a fact of life. But I will not be paralyzed by this fear or die from it if I remember that *God can be trusted.*

Eugenia Price, writing in *Just As I Am,*[1] states:

I grow afraid, just as you do. But my fear, even of the death of a loved one (most difficult of all for me), lives and grows only as long as I turn to other people with it; only as long as I try to overcome it myself. It is cast out (the unhealthy, destructive fear—not the circumstance) when I deliberately remember Jesus.

However, the woman who lets the roaring lion of fear take over in her world will show this fear first in her walk and arm movements; then in her eyes or the expression on her face. Consider this hypothetical Christian woman. She has just heard her doctor diagnose her problem as "breast cancer." She cannot move. Her previous anxiety and general feeling of apprehension has now changed to real, big-time fear. She is in a stunned, paralyzed position. She denies the truth of what he's saying even as she listens to the words of her concerned doctor. When she finally tries to leave his office, she finds she's severely limited in her ability to make her legs work. She has suddenly become rather uncoordinated, and the simple act of leaving his office has become a monumental chore. She reaches for the door handle, but misses on the first try. She's aware that it's becoming harder to breathe.

Still in shock, she finds her way to the parking lot and feels the muscles stiffening and becoming rigid. She drives home trying to pull herself together and rehearsing how she will tell her family. If the lion of fear is large enough,

---

[1] Zondervan Publishing House, Grand Rapids, Michigan

she will wait hours or even days. In any case, by the time she has regained enough courage to tell them, the family has already guessed that something is seriously wrong. After that, her every waking moment is filled with fearful thoughts. She is mauled to a pulp by the lion of fear and temporarily she forgets that God can be trusted. Eventually she may even close her mind to surgery or refuse to consider any other treatment, but her fear cripples her and refuses to let her think logically or move in any direction.

Now let's say this woman's fear is of a less serious nature than cancer ... such as her fear of driving on the freeway or that she is terrified of flying. Then she might not want to get into a car, or she might refuse to board a plane. Her whole life can easily retreat into a steel-reinforced rut. The fear can turn into a phobia where the fear (of whatever or whomever) controls her every movement and thought.

In literature, Seneca writes that the wife of Hercules says of Lyches, "His mind is like he walks." When fear grips our minds and emotions, our every physical move reflects it.

One of the first ingredients of beauty and graciousness in a woman is a cool, relaxed, prepared countenance. The woman of true beauty usually looks as if she can calmly handle anything from a house afire to a glass of milk that was spilled on her new carpeting. But, this prerequisite of charm can be completely obliterated by the lion of fear.

Let's look at what fear does to our faces.

Just as fear restricts any relaxed movement and paralyzes the mind and body, it also hardens facial expressions into frozen masks. If our fear is great, we rarely find anything to smile about, and all others see it in our cold, rather sterile facial expressions. Nothing can make our faces light up in expectation, and nothing will soften our doleful look, and, believe me, nothing ages our faces as fast as fear.

Perhaps none of the fears I've already mentioned have attacked you, but I am going to list a few of my fears and some that other women have disclosed to me. Some are major threats; others are rather trivial; but all are *genuine*, and we must *never* minimize someone's fears—even our own—for they are *real*. Do some of these sound distressingly familiar? Like the fear of ...

1. Wondering what others (my husband, mother-in-law, neighbor, boss, peers) will say or think.
2. Traveling, driving, or flying alone.
3. Discovering cancer in any degree or quantity.
4. Having any incurable disease or discovering that a loved one has a slowly deteriorating terminal illness.
5. Being a widow.
6. Being a divorcee.
7. Dying.
8. Losing a child either to drugs, alcohol, accident, or disease.
9. Not having anyone left in your family to love or need you.
10. Suspecting your husband is having an extramarital affair.
11. Failing (at marriage, raising children, at a job, or with some responsibility).
12. Being disappointed in people *again*.
13. Bankruptcy.
14. Seeing a live snake, lizard, and/or spiders.
15. Growing old ungracefully or suffering from Altzimer's disease.
16. Being lonely and isolated from family and friends.
17. Pregnancy.
18. Not being pregnant.

19. Being caught in an immoral or illegal act.
20. Living with the memories of sexual or physical abuse in your childhood.
21. Dealing with problems or conflicts in relationships.
22. Change.
23. Making a decision.
24. Losing your mind or having to admit to emotional or mental problems.
25. Being rejected and abandoned by people you thought were your friends.

I've left space here for you to add your own special fears, and I encourage you to compile your personal list with directness and objective honesty. After you've added your own fears, then go back over my list and check any that may be apparent in your life . . . no matter how large or slight the fear may be.

It is very important now to carefully study your list because there are two main things we love to do with our fears. One is to deny the lion's existence. The second is to run away from him as fast as our minds can carry us and look frantically for a hiding place.

David did not deny that he was well acquainted with the lion of fear and after he admitted that "stark fear overpowered him," he went on to say, "I would fly to the far off deserts and stay there. I would flee to some refuge from all this storm" (Psalm 55:7-8).

His desire to run and hide from his fears has an all too familiar ring to it.

There seems to be an ostrich-like quality about the way we run or hide from our fears, and no end to the ways in which we fantasize about them . . . perhaps,

We turn to alcohol and drink too much.

We take tranquilizers, sleeping tablets, or pep pills.

We go to bed with a pseudo or psychosomatic illness.

We spend much time analyzing our childhood miseries.

We sit for hours with glazed eyes before a television set.

We go on a reading kick and read one book after another.

We flirt with the opposite sex.

We concentrate all our efforts on making money.

We develop compulsive buying habits.

We join one organization after another.

We develop all sorts of mental mechanisms which prevent us from recognizing the basic problems within . . . all in the frantic effort to drown out the roaring of the lion of fear.

New techniques of escape are constantly being developed. New medicines are flooding the market to enable us to endure this fearful modern world in which we live.

Taking the First Step

"But how in the world can I cope with these personal fears?" you ask. If you've honestly and realistically listed your fears—big ones and little ones—you've just taken the first step in dealing with the lion. Jesus never said we'd be exempt from having problems and fears. In fact, in John 16:33 He said the opposite, "I have told you this so that you will have peace of heart and mind. Here on earth you will have many trials and sorrows but cheer up, for I have overcome the world" (TLB).

Most professional people, ministers, psychologists, and doctors agree that until you find out what ails you, you cannot be cured. Good mental and physical health begins by admitting and then accepting all the facts of our lives—including the unpleasant, the conflicting, or the ugly situations.

Taking the Second Step

The second step in coping with fear is found in asking, "Who is the author of fear?" For it is not enough to honestly pinpoint our fear. We must find out where it originates and stop it at the source. Remember, *God does not give fear:*

"For God hath not given us the spirit of fear" (2 Timothy 1:7 KJV). Our Bible explicitly states that God is love . . . and that perfect love casts out all fear (1 John 4:8,18 KJV).

Paul is puzzled by the Christians he observed in Galatia and writes, "You were getting along so well. Who has interfered with you to hold you back from following the truth? It certainly isn't God who has done it, for He is the one who has called you to freedom in Christ" (Galatians 5:7).

When we hear the first little ping of a fearful thought sounding off in our brains, we need to remember instantly that it is not from God!

Hal Lindsey, in his brilliant but scary book, *Satan Is Alive and Well on Planet Earth*, gives super-intelligent Satan the credit for inventing the power of suggestion, and he brands it as the cleverest of ways to attack us. It is highly possible that Satan knows the full name and social security number of every born-again Christian, and he has written it very carefully down in his book of books.

I believe that Satan is acutely aware that he cannot take Christ away from us or steal our salvation like a pickpocket in a crowd, but I also believe he will do his best to neutralize us into defeated, fatigued, ugly specimens of Christianity.

Satan is capable of finding our particular panic button and pressing it for all he's worth. Your fear might be the big one about breast cancer or a little one like being afraid of driving on busy freeways, but he may find it and use it as his biggest weapon for damaging your sound mental health, confident outward composure, and victorious Christian living.

Sometimes when our fear buttons are pushed, instead of paralyzing us it seems to rally us to fight. So we jump in and make all kinds of New Year's resolutions. We turn over all sorts of new leaves and sincerely make a determined effort to win. However without asking God's help, without realizing the Holy Spirit could be in control of our lives, we spin our wheels and drive in endless, fruitless circles. And of course this is exactly what the enemy of our soul wants. In fact, it fits in perfectly with his battle plan. He wants us to think we live and fight alone, completely alone.

He can plant a fear (sometimes only the suggestion of a fear), and then sit back and watch us wear ourselves to a frazzle fighting it! We are an easy victory for him, particularly if he can get us to spend all our waking, and most of our sleeping, hours troubled with the fear of today or tomorrow. Don't let him or anyone else rob you of one of your most priceless possessions: time.

Remember, too, Satan used Scripture to tempt even Jesus, so you'll be no exception to his rule. He twisted God's words to Eve in the very beginning of time, and she fell for it.

How can you tell the difference between Satan's suggestions and God's? Here's a basic rule of thumb:

If the thought is

> honest—not scrambled in any way
> pure—no ulterior motives
> kind and good—not destructive

it is almost always from the Lord. But, if the thought is

> a lie—even a little one
> a deception—the truth twisted ever so slightly
> a destructive suggestion—that will hurt

it is probably a "popped-in-suggestion" from Satan.

When I've been attacked by the lion of fear during the last few years, I've phoned my friend, Clare. She is wise in the things of God, perceptive, and rarely, even in the face of panic-filled times, seems to lose her God-given sense of humor.

I'll phone and say, "Clare, could I have some of your time and share my fear and panic about such and such?"

"Yes . . . " comes back her good-humored answer, "but only thirty seconds of panic, okay?"

The Lord knows we will have all kinds of anxieties and fears, but maybe we ought to seriously think more in terms of dwelling on them for thirty seconds only. God's got better things for our time than our stewing, fighting, and hassling the invisible lion of fear. Satan would snag us all on this point. Let's be aware of exactly who the enemy really is here so we can take appropriate measures against him.

Taking the Third Step

The third step in coping with our fears is determined by who we let control our lives. It always comes down to a matter of the will. *You* decide.

Paul talks of people who are still under the control of their old sinful natures. He says they can never please God. Then he talks to the new Christians and joyously announces, "But you are not like that. You are controlled by your new nature if you have the Spirit of God living in you" (Romans 8:9).

The right answers to living with our fears are found within our own souls. The secret of victory and of having God's fragrant beauty in our lives and on our faces is not to be found in our struggling alone but in our willing surrender to Christ of the fear that gnaws at us. By using our wills, we can choose who controls, who dominates, and who wins; Satan or Christ.

If your husband or child is late getting home from school or work and you begin to get anxious about their safety and wellbeing, tell that to the Lord. Quiet yourself before God and try to listen to His soft voice of wisdom and reason within yourself. Remember, when we tell the Lord about our fears, it is not an idle chant or well-rehearsed litany. It's a prayer-need. We shouldn't be surprised to hear from our Heavenly Father in one way or another. *Act* then on what you hear from Him. You might feel a gentle peace . . . then act on it . . . relax. You might feel you should call someone to check for information . . . act on that . . . call. And when you've done as much as you feel you should, commit that loved one to the Lord.

You can be sure of this: if God is going to do the big thing we fear at a time like this (death by some kind of accident), He can be trusted, and He will not take our loved one home one minute sooner or later than He decides. Our lives and times are in God's hands. He is in control of the universe. Don't let Satan blow your mind with false fears and imagined tragedies.

Peter vividly warns us about the enemy that would control and destroy us when he states, "Be careful, watch out for attacks from Satan, your great enemy. He prowls around like a hungry, roaring lion, looking for some victim to tear apart. Stand firm when he attacks. Trust the Lord" (1 Peter 5:8-9).

I think the Lord would have us learn a lesson from Daniel on trusting God and committing our fears to Him. Remember Daniel? He was the man who was dropped down into a den full of roaring, hungry lions. When anyone else was thrown down, the hungry lions probably gobbled them up before they had a chance to hit the bottom of the den (Daniel 6:24). Dying was no imagined fear, it was very real to Daniel. Yet, he was so convinced his life and times were in God's hands that he decided to trust and commit this death-fear to his all-seeing, all-caring God ... *without* knowing *how* God would or would not intervene.

What astounds me most about this story is the thought that when Daniel was with those lions, he should have been absolutely petrified with fear. Yet, I believe that he was so relaxed and at peace that he went to sleep. The next morning, Scripture tells us, "Not a scratch was found on him, because he believed in His God" (Daniel 6:23).

The lion of fear need not vandalize our inner beauty, destroy the mobility of our system, or harden the lines on our face. I think if we take these three steps in regard to fear we'll be closer to the beautiful, glowing women God would have us to be.

1.   We need to spread our fears honestly before the Lord on a list and leave the list with Him. Select a shelf or table. Put our daily fears on it. Leave it alone. Stand back and let the Lord be the keeper of the shelf. The next day, when we want to think about that fear, refuse to go to the shelf; don't take the fear down and hold it. It doesn't belong to us now. Let the Lord have it. "Let Him have all your worries and cares, for He is always thinking about you and watching everything that concerns you" (1 Peter 5:7).

2.   We need to know our enemy is Satan. He is the author of all fearful thoughts. God does not remind us of our fear. Satan does, and he'll continue to use the power of suggestion if we let him. In 1 Peter 8:5 the apostle is explicit . . . "Be careful—watch out for attacks from Satan, your great enemy . . ." (TLB).

3.   We need to decide exactly who we will allow to control our mind, soul, and body. The Word of God reminds us that, "Greater is He that is in you, than he that is in the world" (1 John 4:4 KJV). So remember, Satan is not in first place. Jesus knows the exact depth and width of each Satan-inspired fear.

If Christ is our Lord and Savior, then He can be trusted. He is able. Take heart. All things *will* work together for good (Romans 8:28) even if we can't see it or figure it out right here and now. God—not Satan—is in control. He can give us all the strength and energy we'll ever need in combating the fears of a broken world. We'll come out like Daniel—not a single lion's scratch to be found!

Additional scripture references for this chapter.

(Letters following each reference indicate which translation: TLB—The Living Bible; RSV—Revised Standard Version; ML—Modern Language; Amp.—Amplified.)

God	Genesis 15:1 KJV
	Genesis 26:24 KJV
	Numbers 14:9 TLB
	Psalm 71:20 TLB
	Psalm 62:6 TLB
	Acts 27:23-25 KJV
	2 Timothy 1:7 KJV, TLB
	1 Peter 5:7 RSV
Satan	Ephesians 6:10-17 TLB
	James 4:7 KJV
	1 Peter 5:8 TLB
	1 John 5:19 ML
Fear	Psalm 23:4 KJV
	Psalm 49:5 TLB
	Isaiah 8:13 TLB
	Isaiah 43:1-5 KJV
	Luke 8:50 KJV
	1 John 4:18 KJV
Obedience	Joshua 1:7-9 TLB
	James 4:17 KJV
Inner Beauty	Psalm 94:19 TLB
	Psalm 46:1-5 TLB
	John 14:1 TLB
	John 14:27 TLB
	John 16:33 KJV
	1 Peter 1:2 TLB

THREE

Fadeless Beauty of Faith and Face

If we give our fears to Christ and keep on giving them to Him when they come, as I described in the previous chapter, we are well on our way to achieving a measure of Christ's beauty!

However, it's a fact of life that when we take something out or away from our lives we leave a hole, a space, or a vacancy. We always need something to replace the emptiness. What do you think the divine replacement for *fear* is? I may be wrong but I believe the opposite of fear is a *positive working faith*.

Fear is one of the most destructive emotions in the world. It can spread from neighbor to neighbor, mate to mate, and parents to children quicker than the black plague, *but so can faith*! Beautiful faith, even tiny underdeveloped faith, can move mountains, can spread peace, can give a glimpse of hope to all it touches.

Fear is based on the unknown—what we *think* might happen. It is possible to have today's fears all safely tucked away in God's steady hand, but what about tomorrow's catastrophic fears? Can faith cover tomorrow too? I believe the answer is a resounding, yes!

"Faith," the writer of Hebrews says, "is the confident assurance that something we want is going to happen. It is the certainty that what we hope for is waiting for us, even though we cannot see it up ahead" (Hebrews 11:1).

I think it's a little irrational to say that we trust and believe God fully with the realities of our lives while we still live in a continual state of fear. We must not let fear control our moves and thoughts.

Fear hovers in some Christian women like a low-grade fever. This "fever" is never high enough to hospitalize them, but I've seen the flush of fear just under the surface. Sometimes I've seen my own flush when I've looked into a mirror.

God and prolonged fear are rather incompatible. Fear and faith are at opposite ends of the pole. A woman of faith cannot be a woman of continual fear.

If we are women of fear, we will see our future as a frightening menace. We will end up being afraid of our own shadow. The woman of faith, on the other hand, believes that while she may not understand all the intricate workings of God in her problems and trouble, she can trust Him and views her future with confidence and hope. Whether her faith is brand new and mustard-seed-sized, or older and fills a suitcase, she knows, "Anything is possible if you have faith" (Mark 9:23).

I always flinch a little when I hear a Christian woman say, "I'm so afraid of what will happen next," then sheepishly she adds, "I guess I need more faith."

Paul tells us, "God hath dealt to every man the measure of faith" (Romans 12:3 KJV). What we need is not more faith but to use what we have! Our potential for faith is limitless.

When the Bible talks about faith, one of the clearest concepts involves our coming to Christ *just as we are*. We are not to clean up our lives, get all dressed up in our finest and then go to God. No! We are to bring Him our doubts, our confusion, our failures, and, yes, our fears from wherever we are. God does not lie. He is the Good News. He is real, and He, so long ago, chose to love us first. Read it in Ephesians 1:4. I love The Living Bible's paraphrase of this verse.

Faith in Christ is not a human trait like courage or trustworthiness. It's not even an attitude of heart or a state of mind which some women have while others do not. It is a supernatural phenomenon that comes in varying degrees after we have heard about Jesus and God's Good News.

Paul says, "Yet faith comes from listening to this Good News—the Good News about Christ" (Romans 10:17).

We can never please God without faith and "without depending on Him" as Hebrews 11:6 adds.

Previously, I stated that fear paralyzes us. It robs us of relaxation and poise. Faith works with exactly the opposite effect. Faith in Jesus can restore the calmness of mind our body needs. It can untie knotted nerves above the tummy area and loosen those tense back muscles. Faith can allow us to lie down in safety and can assure us a good night's rest, even though fears often loom larger at night. We need, however, to choose faith *over* fear.

Faith enables us to pray before falling asleep:
"Lord, I give you my cluttered conscious mind ... it's fears and joys, its failures and successes. Here it is for You to take and hold. Now I give You my subconscious mind. You know I've no control over the passing patterns of thought or the dreams I might dream tonight, but You made me, and I will trust You. I go to sleep safe in Your keeping. Good night, dear Lord."

Our daughter, Laurie, was just about nine years old when her fear of spiders really took over. She seemed able to cope with it during the day. She even got to the place where she could objectively examine a specimen without coming completely unglued, but at night it was another story.

Each evening she would sleep for one or two hours, and then the nightmares would begin. I'd hear her thrashing about, and crying out and I'd rush into her room to find her sitting or kneeling in bed, frantically brushing thousands of imaginary spiders and ants out of the sheets and blankets. Putting the light on and showing her the empty bed was of some comfort to her, but fear had so emotionally exhausted her that returning to sleep was almost impossible.

Week after week her screaming woke the entire family, and all of us began suffering fatigue from those disastrous nightmares.

I seemed to be able to help Laurie cope with her conscious fears during the day, but I hadn't the faintest idea of how to handle the subconscious ones at night.

Finally, after six weeks of interrupted rest, she cried out one night and I ran to her room for the umpteenth time. I was at my wits end but determined to help her give the Lord these fears and fill up the vacancy that was left. I did not turn on her bedroom light. I simply grabbed her by the shoulders and in one or two quick maneuvers pulled her down into bed, brought the covers up around her shoulders, and out loud—in a strong, rather commanding voice, I prayed by faith, "Dear Lord, You know Laurie keeps dreaming about spiders. Please take these spider dreams away from her right now and give her good dreams instead." I waited a moment and then hopefully prayed, "Thank you, Lord, for the good dream she is going to have. Amen."

With that, I tucked the blanket under her chin, kissed the little freckle on her nose, and went to bed.

It didn't dawn on me that apparently all of us, including Laurie, had slept the rest of the night through until I was putting bread into the toaster the next morning.

Laurie's cheery and rested little voice behind me said, "Guess what?"

When I turned, there she stood all smiles and she said, "I had the best dream *ever*!"

"Really? What was it?" I asked.

"I dreamed you gave me a quarter and you said, 'Go into that candy store and buy whatever you want!' "

About a month later, I realized we'd all been sleeping the whole night through. "Laurie-Honey", are you having any more spider nightmares?"

"Nope," she answered.

"Did they just stop and all go away, completely?" I questioned.

"No, not all at once," she said. "A couple of nights after you prayed for me, I woke up from another spider dream. I was going to call you, but instead I just prayed, 'Dear Lord, take this dream away and give me the good kind,' and He did . . . so I didn't wake you."

The faith that God could take care of a real fear (even a subconscious nightmare) made our Laurie a shining, sparkling little girl that morning. I'll never forget how beautiful and how rested and relaxed she looked. It really showed.

My mother was beautiful because of her faith too, and she continually replaced fear by faith. When one of women's greatest fears—the fear of cancer—became a reality in her life, she seized upon the experience and her faith grew to enormous proportions.

After the removal of one breast, she was having cobalt treatments at U.C.L.A. Medical Center when lumps were discovered in the other breast. Because of a number of factors, including the size of the new tumors, a second mastectomy was ruled out.

Mother or Mrs. Miller-Honey, as she was called, was a favorite with doctors, nurses, and attendants alike. A doctor, the chief of radiology, told a large gathering of visiting doctors from all over the world about her. He stressed in his lecture that when a cancer patient had *faith* like Mrs. Miller, he and the medical staff were prepared to see anything happen. It could be a brief, temporary remission of the disease or even a dramatic, miraculous recovery. "The key," he said, "is the patient's faith in God." He went on to warn, "If a patient has no faith at all, the course of events is pretty predictable. The patient is dead already." Twenty-three years later Norman Cousins' book *Head First: The Biology of Hope* documents and confirms exactly what the doctors, nurses and our family all saw in my mother's remarkable faith.

My mother and I talked much about replacing fear with faith and one day after a cobalt treatment at the hospital, she excitedly told me what had just happened.

She had been placed on a gurney, one of those narrow hospital beds with wheels, and rolled into a hallway to await her treatments. The nurses all knew of Mother's extraordinary faith, so they often deliberately parked her bed near any patient who was despondent or upset. That day had been no exception, and the patient beside her was sobbing as if her heart would break.

Mother reached across the little space between them and asked gently, "What's the matter? What's wrong?"

The woman turned her head and faced Mother with a rather disgusted look. "Are you kidding? ... What do you mean, what's wrong? Look where I am ... I've got cancer!" she said angrily.

"So do I," said Mother.

"Yes," continued the woman, "but I had surgery for the removal of one breast, and now I've got lumps on the other side."

"So have I," came the quiet response.

"But that's not all," she countered. "These treatments make me violently ill."

"I know. Me too," my mother said. But the woman continued.

"Besides all that, I'm in my fifties and I think I'm going to die!" Now, the woman was almost shouting.

"I think I am too," came Mother's reflective answer.

At this point, the woman rose up on one elbow to get a better look at my mother, and her words hissed and sizzled. "Well, then, how can you lie there so G— D— peaceful?"

My mother said she wasn't shocked at the woman's profanity because she understood the stark fear that prompted and propelled it. She didn't give her a lecture on the sin of using God's name in vain. She simply jumped in with both feet to the heart of the basic problem. "Have you tried praying?" she asked gently.

The woman settled back down, heaved a frustrated sigh and said, "*Of course I've prayed!* I've even gone to every church in our area. I've prayed everything from Christian Scientist to Buddhist back to Baptist prayers, and you know what? None of them worked."

"I know why," my mother said.

The woman, still up on her elbow, was looking over at mother and really listening. "You do? Why?"

"You didn't pray with faith. You must pray with faith . . . believing God will hear. You've got a terrible need in your life. Someone told you to go see the King and petition Him to help you. But without preparation or invitation, you barged into the King's throne room. You yelled, `Okay, King, I've got cancer and you'd better do something about it. You gave it to me, so you'd better take it back!' Then, because you were so sure He wouldn't help you, you stormed out of His palace without even waiting for a reply. You told your friend and relatives, 'See, I told you so! I went to the King, and He didn't hear me or help me!'" The woman listened intently and my mother went on.

"How different it would have been had you humbly gone before the King of all kings, Jesus, poured out your heart, confessed your sins, and then told him about your unbearable needs, *in faith* asking Him to go with you through this valley, *in faith* confessing your need of strength to bear this cancer, and *in faith* believing that He would *never* leave or forsake you."

The woman's belligerence began to wash away with the tears that were streaming down her face. She reached over the space between the gurneys and grabbed my mother's hand.

Mother ended with, "You think your essential problem is to get rid of cancer, but what you really need is Jesus."

Through her tears the woman said, "Pray for me, please—*now!*" This story was related to me once more, several weeks after my mother's death, by the head nurse. She gave me a postscript about the woman. The nurse said, "We saw a fantastic change in that patient after your mother prayed for her. She lost her depression, in fact, she was like a new woman."

My mother was one of those exceptionally beautiful women who dared to pray daily the prayer of faith. Her faith became stronger and more real with time because of the results she saw.

I can't remember the name of the story, but according to a *Reader's Digest* article I once read, no scientist has ever seen an atom. Yet every scientist believes in atoms because he sees and ascertains the results of atomic energy. I think faith is like that—we've never seen it, but we've seen the *results* of faith.

The Apostle Peter tells women to be beautiful on the inside because that's a lasting thing and very precious to God. He says, "That kind of deep beauty was seen in the saintly women of old, who trusted God and fitted in with their husbands' plans" (1 Peter 3:5).

My mother's "deep beauty" went hand in hand with her faith and her unfailing trust in Jesus, her dearest friend.

By faith we can see Jesus. We can, by faith, see that He came

"To bind up the broken hearted,
To proclaim liberty to the captives . . .
To comfort all that mourn . . .
To give unto them
    Beauty for ashes,
    The oil of joy for mourning,
    The garment of praise for the spirit of heaviness."
        (Isaiah 61:1-3 KJV)

What an exchange! Think of it! Coming to Christ just as we are and having Him give us beauty for our ashes.

Edna St. Vincent Milay wrote:

Man then has not invented God;
He has developed faith,
To meet a God already there![1]

We have just spent considerable time looking together into God's spiritual mirror. We are aware, or should be, that any deep or lasting beauty inside us is based on the absence of perpetual fears and on a never-ending growth of faith.

---

[1] From *Conversations at Midnight*, Harper & Brothers, New York.

But let's look now at the glass mirror above our dresser or our bathroom sink and see what we have going for us on the outside. What do we see? What do other people see when they look at us? What inner beauty, if any, does our face reflect? What's our best facial feature? What's our hair like? Do I wear makeup, or, if I don't, should I start? These thoughts and many others will probably arise as we look into our reflection.

While I was writing this chapter, my mailman brought a letter from a twenty-three-year-old wife and mother. She had read one of my books and was writing to thank me for it, but she was also troubled about some things in her life. She asked several questions. One was, "I want to be Christ-centered, but I still find myself interested in how I look and how my hair looks. Is it wrong for a Christian to want to look nice?"

It wasn't the first time someone asked about outward appearances. Neither has it been the last. The answer is absolutely no, there is nothing wrong with a Christian wanting to look nice! When we have received inward beauty for the ashes of our life, it is bound to show on our faces.

Our faith certainly determines the depth of our facial beauty, but we can definitely help or hinder those outward looks. We can ignore them completely or smother them with all kinds of frills, both of which do not enhance our looks.

Your look into the mirror might reveal that you're basically doing what's right for you. Only a tiny push in the right direction may update your hair style, soften a look that has changed with your age, or put to use a new product that's suited to your facial bone structure or coloring. So, keep at it. Don't be afraid to try a new thing or experiment a bit to make the most of your natural looks. I think, without fear of contradiction, the clown-look in makeup is out, but you get my point, I'm sure.

But what if the mirror confirms the suspicion that a lot or most everything is wrong? Skin, hair, and figure all seem to need help? We are very fortunate to live in an age when there are many avenues open to us. The training schools, books, or courses, and the prices of each, differ according to your needs and budget.

The most thorough courses in charm and self-improvement are taught at modeling school.

The beauty expert I mentioned before told me that this type of intensive course is excellent for many women because a professional expert can take a personalized interest in you. She can give you the specific help you need. She's well qualified to help organize your grooming habits. She may be the first person to help you realize your good traits and minimize your flaws—especially the ones you have no control over—big feet, a narrow face, a six feet-two or five-feet-two height.

Many women have discovered an excellent source of help from trained beauty consultants. There are several wonderful cosmetic companies in business who send an expert to your home or to groups in a friend's home to help you personalize your makeup. There's Avon, Mary Kay, and others, including the makeup I've used for years now—Aloette', but find the one that's right for you and your budget.

A good beauty consultant will analyze your face, hair, coloring, bone structure, and even lifestyle to name a few. Then she'll prescribe the "look" that best suits you and truly *is* you.

If you don't want quite this specialized type of attention, there are other opportunities. Some churches have recognized this need and have marvelous courses for women. The girls that come out of that class at one church

I know of are glowingly feminine. Then there are a number of health spas and gyms to restore or reshape your figure. Even in department stores, you can find help. Professional cosmetic sales people can give you a quick facial survey and help you toward balanced beauty. There are also beauty specialty shops like Merle Norman which may be located near you.

To stimulate your thinking, here is a list of some basic ABC's required for outward beauty.

1. *Clean, clean skin*

Basic to all beauty is head-to-toe cleanliness, but it's particularly important with regard to your face. Use cold or warm creams, lotions—anything to get it clean. Most beauty experts feel that soap dries the natural oils and accelerates the aging process, so go easy on soap. Find the cream that works for you and use it! After a good cleaning, you might want to finish off with an astringent. It closes the pores. By the way, keep all beauty supplies (like brushes) clean too.

2. *Sensible makeup foundation*

Few of us have the flawless, unblemished, peaches-and-cream skin I saw yesterday on an eighteen-year-old beauty. Most likely we have red blotches, lines, bone structure irregularities, and, at least once a month, a delicately shaped circle of blue under our eyes.

I personally use Aloette's foundation base, as it covers without looking like a thick layer of paint, and it *suits* me. My daughter has super-sensitive, allergic-to-anything skin, and she uses Loreal or cosmetics that don't irritate the skin. Whatever you choose—a liquid or a cream—in a tube or a jar, a stick or a cake, the main point is to cover blemishes with something that will not turn orange or chalky-white, cause a rash or look like it's an inch thick. Remember too, every face needs some kind of moisturizer, just as a garden needs rain. The older I get, the more I use a moisturizer creme under my foundation makeup.

3. *Sparkling eyes*

Since our eyes are the "windows of our souls," everyone from Aunt Mabel in Podunk to Mollie the fashion model in Paris should give attention to the care and beauty of the eyes. If there are very few women who can go without foundation makeup, there are even fewer who can go eye-less into our world. We are *very* eye conscious.

However, if you are seventeen years old and have large, stunning, blue eyes with long, thick, softly curled black eyelashes, you can skip this part. You don't need any help. But for the rest of us, discover your eyes by starting at the top and working down.

A. Pluck out stray hairs, and thin your eyebrows where it's necessary. You may need to use an eyebrow pencil or brush to fill in some sparse spots, but remember that the harder and darker you lay on that pencil, the harder and darker you look.

B. There are many colors and kinds of eye shadow. Use it sparingly in the daylight hours, but enjoy it for evening. It will add a soft, glowing sparkle to your eyes, and it will usually pick up extra colors that are hidden in the iris of the eye. Your general eye color may be brown or blue, but if you look at your eyes in a magnifying mirror, you'll see all kinds of colors. That's why, when you wear a dress of a certain shade or hue, your eyes seem to change color. Anyway, experiment with colors of eye shadows. Use them sparingly, however, because you're not dressing up to be in a circus. Most of us need someone else to guide us in the eye shadow department. If you wear glasses, as I do, your eye makeup will have to be of deeper color and a little more "made up" to give the right effect.

C. Invest that dollar or two for an eyelash curler. Just as curls around or by your face soften it, so does curling the eyelashes. The look is feathery and pretty. Then use mascara to thicken and darken.

D.   Perhaps you don't have eyelashes long enough to get a curler around. By all means, try wearing false eyelashes. Before you pounce on me for *such* a suggestion, I don't mean you should look cheap or like a girl who wears false eyelashes that are so long one must stand three feet away to avoid getting swept up in their backlash. I'm not suggesting the extreme look in lashes. As a matter of fact, most false lashes need trimming and sizing to fit the individual's eyelid. You might need only the small addition of a demi-lash to give a fuller look. Remember, in order to enhance our looks, we women of today sometimes wear a number of false items: wigs, dentures, and padded bras, to name a few. So, take a good front- and side-view look in the mirror and see if you can enhance the windows of your soul.

4.   *Lips:* To color or not to color?

Ah, here was the great sin of the nineteen twenties and thirties—especially if the lipstick was really out-and-out red. Color in the nineteen forties went to a deep purple-red. In the nineteen fifties, it dissolved into clear reds, but by the middle sixties, it dwindled down to soft whitish pinks and light oranges. In the late nineteen sixties, some regressed to a pure death-like white. Teen-agers looked ghoulish, and older women looked as if they had been dead for days. At the beginning of the nineteen seventies, pale pinks were back—made with new textures. "Frosted and creamy" or "polished and wet" became the look of lipsticks. Since fads tend to repeat themselves every twenty years, I predict that by the end of the nineties we'll be back to dark purple-reds again.

What should *you* wear? Find the shade that softens or flatters your face, and use it to enhance your looks. You need a lipstick that's light and sheer, yet covers completely.

This same advice goes for coloring your cheeks with blush—softness is the rule. The older we get, the more pastel we should use.

One other word on lipstick—try to stay away from applying lipstick or any makeup in a public place. After a meal in a restaurant, church banquet hall, or private home, go to a restroom to restore worn-off makeup, and mend your fences alone! Truly ugly is the woman who gets out her little mirror and crudely goes through all her personal restoration acts in front of everybody. I say this knowing full well there are times when you can't slip out to the restroom, so you just have to sneak some lipstick on *while* you're sitting at the head table at a church banquet and everyone is watching. I know! I know!

5. *Alive hair*

The Bible says the very hairs of our head are numbered. If our hair is that important to the Lord, then surely there are a number of things we should do in caring for and maintaining our hair.

We should keep it clean. Use a PH balanced shampoo and a conditioning rinse. Don't skimp on either item. You could end up with permanently damaged hair. Mousse or hair "shapers" are great too.

Seek out a hairdresser or even a good men's barber for a haircut, trim, or style change as often as needed. If it's been two years since you had someone change or really work on your hair, you are past due! Make an appointment tomorrow. If you can't afford professional services, ask around; you may find someone who knows a talented teenager who is a whiz with the scissors or home permanent kits.

This mini-beauty course of ABC requirements for enhancing outward beauty is *very* basic, but it might mean the difference between confirming and denying the faith that is within you.

It would be wonderful if we could stand at a distance and see ourselves as God and mankind see us. Maybe we would immediately be able to properly evaluate our looks. But all we really have is God's mirror (His Word) for our faith and our dressing room mirror for our face. Let's use them both enthusiastically to be the beautiful women of faith and face God intended.

Additional Scripture references for this chapter.

Christ	1 Peter 1:21 - TLB
	Proverbs 22:17-19 - TLB
Faith Working in us	Psalm 4:8 - TLB
	Psalm 32:8 - TLB
Trust	Psalm 46:1-3 - KJV
	Psalm 55:17-23 - KJV
	Psalm 91 - KJV
	Psalm 94:19 - KJV, TLB
Beauty	Genesis 29:17 - KJV
	1 Samuel 16:12 - KJV
	1 Samuel 25:3 - KJV
	Esther 2:7 - KJV
	Psalm 90:17 - KJV
	Isaiah 61:3 - TLB
	2 Corinthians 2:18

FOUR

Worry: A Scampering Mouse

The world is full of worry,
Everlasting worry;
Worry about this and worry about that,
Worry a little and worry a lot,
Worry with nothing to worry about,
Just worry, worry, worry.
                    C. T. Weigle

A tense, fidgety, overwrought young woman did not sit across from me on my couch; she nervously perched. Her shoulders never touched the back cushions, and she moved restlessly along the outer edges of the couch as she talked. It is the way distraught and emotionally uptight people sit. They do not trust the chair or couch, they've been fooled before, so they perch, ready to get up in a moments notice, expecting the worst to happen.

Worry is a mouse,
A small scampering thing
With sharp tiny feet
That scurries over our soul.

60

Quite visibly, the mouse of worry not only was scampering over the young woman's soul, but over her face, her hands, and her body motions, as well. All the "worries" in her life created an edgy, tense person.

She talked on and on—non-stop. Often she interrupted herself to digress from one subject to another. Her comments were defensive, often critical, and occasionally filled with self-pity. Once in a while, her speech was punctuated by a nervous, high-pitched laugh, which was accompanied by a weird facial expression. Her restless hands tugged at her skirt, then nervously twisted a strand of hair. Her slender fingers ended in blunt stumps of bitten-off nails, The young and probably once-pretty face was a distorted, portrait of conflicts and inner anguish.

The effects and consequences of worry were evident in every area of her being.

Let me list some of those consequences, for I see them in myself and in any woman who lets the mouse of worry scamper unchecked through her soul.

1. *Worry borrows*

It's a disease of the future. It borrows the unknown trouble of tomorrow. The worrier loses the beautiful spirit of hope because worry paints such a gloomy, shocking, dreadful picture of the future. Worriers become deeply troubled about something that very well may never take place, or they worry about something that happened thirty years ago that can't possibly be changed now.

2. *Worry broods*

It simmers on some back burner in the depths of a our minds. It limits activity and curtails creativity. It is like a brood hen sitting on her nest, for if she broods long enough, she will hatch a flock of troubles—real or imagined.

3. *Worry is a mental burden*

Seneca, many centuries ago, said, "The mind that is

anxious about the future is miserable." A woman's worry affects her mental ability to act wisely and severely limits her mental power to think logically and clearly. Her mind locks into a standard position: *miserable*. I wonder what David was worried about when he wrote, "My mind is filled with apprehension and with gloom" (Psalm 6:3).

This state of mind might not be too terrible if it affected only the worrier, but it is highly contagious! Soon others catch it, and the woman who worries finds she has infected her family, business associates, and friends as well. She wonders why she has a hard time keeping relationships. She also wonders why so few people ever *really* ask, "How are you?".

4.   *Worry is a physical burden*

There seems to be little doubt that worry *kills*. It may not be swift as cancer, but it is just as deadly. Worry acts like

> a poison in the blood,
> a drain on inner vitality,
> a stiffening in the joints,
> a hardening of the arteries,

and very often it is the cause of an ulcer. (Experts in the medical professions say that chronic worriers are far more likely to have cancer.)

A woman can experience real pain from mental worries. Ralph Waldo Emerson once spoke of " ... the torments of pain you endured, from evils that never arrived."

5.   *Worry robs*

It steals the magic sparkle from a woman's eyes. It takes the alive, alert quality from her appearance and substitutes dullness in its place. Worry confiscates a woman's ability to smile and permanently etches a frown into the lines of her face, adding years to her looks.

6.   *Worry is a habit*

Life is full of habits—good and bad—but a worrying woman is often so close to her habit that she does not see it for the bad one it is. The habit of worry holds a death-like grip on her whole life.

7.   *Worry is absolutely useless*

Worrying never helps any situation. It blinds a woman to possible solutions and makes her real problems tougher and more complicated. It always clouds or muddies the issues involved.

In *Letters To His Son*, Lord Chesterfield said, "I recommend you to take care of the minutes, for the hours will take care of themselves." But the worrying woman is too bound—worrying about her problems—to take care of either the minutes or the hours.

8.   *Worry is definitely a sin*

While worry is a natural, human emotion that we all experience, it becomes definitely a sin when we let it rule our thoughts. It clearly reveals our lack of faith in God's ability to work out the details of our lives. It reflects a verdict against God's faithfulness, and brings reproach on His name, because it means the worrier really doesn't think God has a solution to her problem.

Once, when I was talking with my mother about this very thing, the sin of worrying, she said, "You're right, worry is a sin for the Christian woman. But the unsaved, the non-Christian ... ah, there's a different story. They have a right, almost a duty, to worry, because they have no Christ to rely on as we do!"

The young woman who twisted and turned on my couch that day typified many women I've seen over the past few years. I'm no stranger to the worry written all over her because I've seen it in my own life and in my own family. Let me tell you about my twin aunts.

Ever since I can remember, I loved my Aunt Harriet and Aunt Hortense. Over the years I learned one lesson after another from these two darlings. They are both with the Lord now but even when they were well into their seventies, they were beautiful women. When they were young girls, they won one of the first national toothpaste "smile" contests! They were not only identical in looks, but they shared identical tastes and preferences.

Aunt Hortense would go to town, purchase some article, perhaps clothing or shoes, and come home to find that Aunt Harriet had bought the same article from the same store and the same salesperson on the very same day!

Both aunts married and lived most of their lives in the same town and neighborhood, separated by only a few blocks. A few years ago they both became widows.

Over the years, something happened to their "identical" look. It was hard to explain because they still looked alike physically, yet the "inner" essence of fragrance in one was very different from the other. Aunt Harriet looked older (and not by twenty minutes, either!), more depressed, strained, and tense. Aunt Hortense had an alive, alert quality that instantly drew you to her.

Once we (as a family) accepted the twins as they were, with their very opposite personalities, they became a delightful study in contrasts and remained so until their deaths.

Whenever I'd see them at a family get-together, I'd have trouble telling them apart for a minute or so, and then I'd take a closer look and just listen and, sure enough, one would say something and the whole matter of identity was quickly settled.

After I moved to California from Michigan, they wrote me priceless letters. Their letters always arrived within two or three days of each other and both covered the same subjects. However, there was an amazing difference in their attitudes. I have prepared composite letters which typify their correspondence through the years: Here is Aunt Harriet's letter ...

Dear Joyce,

We are having a terrible snowstorm. It's going to go into a blizzard. No lettuce this spring, and the farmers say this weather is to blame.

Your Uncle Walter couldn't drive to work today, so he had to walk all that way. He can't stand too much of that cold wind and those icy streets.

Mrs. Brondage, down the street, slipped just last week and fractured her hip. Not two days before, I *told* her that would happen.

I'm not feeling good at all, so I can't get out to prayer meeting. Even when I do go, I don't see too many there. Seems like people aren't interested in spiritual things anymore. I've quit teaching my Sunday School class. Those little children make me too nervous for words.

Uncle Greg flew to Chicago yesterday. I hope he doesn't crash. You can't trust those airplanes. Just read the newspaper—airplanes crash all the time.

Well, I've got to close as I want to hear the 6 o'clock news. My, things are in terrible shape all over the world. I wonder how long all of this can go on. It's awful.

Love,
Aunt Harriet

Soon after I read her letter, Aunt Hortense's epistle arrived:

Dearest Joyce,

You should see the beautiful snow! It's been coming down for hours and everything is white and sparkly.

We've had a pretty cold winter so far, but you know that makes great apples and cherries later on!

Cars aren't doing too well on the streets, so your Uncle Walter had to walk to work. I think that's great. He needs the fresh air and exercise.

Mrs. Brondage, our neighbor, slipped and fell last week. Today I took her some homemade soup. She seemed pleased, and much better.

I haven't been too well this year, but I'm able to get out to prayer meeting once in a while. There are not too many out but the Lord said, "Where two or three are gathered, there am I in the midst," so the Lord comes on Wednesday, even when we don't. I'm still teaching my Sunday School class after all these years. My, how I love those dear little tykes.

Your Uncle Greg flew to Chicago yesterday. Isn't that something? Just think, from here to there in a few minutes—what a wonder.

Must close. I want to catch the news. My, when you hear all that's going on in the world today—wars, murders, and what have you—aren't you glad you know Jesus? And that He is in control and cares for us? I am!

Love,
Aunt Hortense

All their letters were like vivid maps. In great detail they showed exactly how and where each one lived out their lives.

Once when I was back East on a speaking engagement, to my joy, my relatives decided to have a family reunion picnic. The twin aunts were the last to arrive. I saw them get out of a car, so I ran across the park lawn to greet them. As I got closer, it dawned on me how much they *still* looked alike. I laughed because I couldn't tell them apart. When I reached them, I hugged the first aunt I came to, and said, "Whom do I have here?"

My aunt gave me a great big smile and playfully refused to tell me her name. Out of the corner of my eye I saw the sober look on the other twin's face and heard her sum up the whole thing rather well with, "I'm the *other* one."

Instantly, I knew I was holding and hugging Aunt Hortense. Her optimistic, God-will-take-care-of-everything spirit had kept her warm and vibrant. She was bending toward me while Aunt Harriet was straightening up stiffly away from me.

That day in the park, I loved watching both of them. The children of my cousins swarmed over Aunt Hortense like bees finding a field of blossoms. Aunt Harriet—worn down by years of worry—coolly remarked, "I don't know how she stands those noisy children climbing all over her!"`

The woman who worries misses all the sunshine of life because she's forever expecting rain. She makes a storm out of a shower, a disaster out of a disappointment. She looks for the day to bring failures and losses and, when it does, she's the first to say, "I told you so!"

No one is immune to worrisome circumstances or problems. Difficult situations confront all of us in one way or another. Sometimes they come upon us with surprising suddenness. This surprise is a kind of numbing, shock experience; and, actually, it can help us at the time. It's nature's way of carrying us through the hardest moment of grief or crisis.

Perhaps you've experienced this: you've been driving on the freeway and have watched an accident happen all around you. You surprise yourself by managing to drive calmly, bravely, even skillfully through it without a scratch. Then, when you're completely safe, you've pulled over to an off ramp and gone completely to pieces.

We seem to survive the worst moments in life with a superior kind of instinctive courage. But afterward—

what then? When the surprise and the numbness pass, worry begins, and we fall apart.

Let me emphasize that it *is* natural to worry. Yet, it is not in God's plan for us to spend our every waking moment worrying over each detail of our lives.

The world in which we live is full of very large problems. Each day brings new issues that must be dealt with. Not one of these issues, big or small, can be solved by the loss of sleep, by tied-up nerves, by headaches, backaches, or by any other companions of worry.

The woman who honestly wants to sweep the mouse of worry out of her soul has got to start right there: with her soul. What is her personal relationship to Jesus? The biggest obstacle to inner beauty in the world today is the lack of peace with God.

Go back for a moment to the young woman on my couch. The basic issue of her relationship with Jesus was where I began when she had finished baring her soul. It was a joyous moment that day when we prayed together and she gave Christ her life. She took the leap over the sin obstacle and was off and running toward God's beauty. She made her peace with God.

She's has never been the same since the basic issue of sin was settled and she was forgiven by God. This woman took a 180 degree turn from tensely anticipating everything to taking life as it comes, with God's peace.

But, worry is a habit. To overcome it, we need to bring the first worry of the morning (and all the little ones that follow) to the Savior's attention. We know that now, since we are God's children, habitual worry is a sin for us. We know, too, that we don't want worrying to come between us and God's loving care.

David knew how important it is to have God's daily forgiveness for sin. He wrote, "I know You get no pleasure from wickedness and cannot tolerate the slightest sin" (Psalm 5:4).

Worry is one of those "slightest sins," but the worry habit can be deeply ingrained.

When this young woman became a Christian, she did not drop her worry automatically. She had been addicted to worry years before she accepted Christ, and it would have continued had she not recognized the issues involved. I'm happy to report that she brought her worry problems to Jesus, with astonishing results.

A bad habit or addiction must be broken and banished in order for faith to have a place to grow. Any habit can be broken—from alcoholism to fingernail biting to a nervous giggle—*if* the possessor of the habit has a real desire to put a stop to it and *if* something constructive is put in its place.

Previously I stated that worry is a mental burden. We need to take our minds (the ones that continue to worry) and begin to use them constructively. We need to look at Proverbs 20:24. It makes great sense. "Since the Lord is directing our steps, why try to understand everything that happens along the way?" The logic of this verse relieves some mental pressure, and almost instantly we can relax in God's peace.

Now, I'm sure you can follow this:

If we believe that God's power can give a man or a woman brains—then we can believe that God's power can govern the brain He made.

If God's power can govern the brain, then it can keep that brain organized, neat, and orderly.

If God's power can make an orderly brain, then it can put worry into the inconspicuous and unimportant corner of our mind where worry belongs. It's like sweeping the kitchen floor until all the dust is in one corner.

If God's power can localize the worry, relegating it to a small heap, then it can also furnish the dustpan that will take worry off the floor of our brain entirely and provide the ash heap on which to toss it! We can enjoy our spic-and-span mind because of God's mighty power at work.

The instant the mouse of worry tries to sneak in, we need to use our minds to believe God completely! Admit Him into our lives completely! Admit the width of His resources, the height of His intellect, and the depth of His love.

Why do you suppose Paul told us so precisely *what* to think on in his letter to the Philippians? I'm sure he knew about the times we tend to think worrisome thoughts. He knew too, that we become whatever we think about. So he wrote down a great mental health principle to think and live by.

He knew if we would concentrate our thinking on

truth,
goodness,
pure and lovely things,
fine and good traits in others,
praise and gratefulness to God,

we'd have very little time for the negative, destructive thinking which worry produces. Also, we'd become like our thoughts. (See Philippians 4:8).

An unknown writer penned the following prayer, and if your life is tied up in knots with the sin of worry, read it carefully. Perhaps as you slowly read it, you can breathe in God's calming beauty; then, exhale the restless tensions of your life. If you will ask God to meet your need and break your habit, He will. He'll replace fretful worries with His very own restful peace.

Slow me down Lord! Ease the pounding of my heart by the quieting of my mind. Steady my hurried pace with a vision of the eternal reach of times. Give me, amidst the confusion of my day, the calmness of the everlasting hills. Break the tension of my nerves and muscles with the soothing music of the singing streams that live in my memory. Help me to know the magical restorative power of sleep. Teach me the art of taking minute vacations . . . of slowing down to look at a flower, to chat with a friend, to pat a dog, to read a few lines from a good book.

Remind me each day of the fable of the hare and the tortoise that I may know that the race is not always to the swift; that there is more to life than increasing its speed. Let me look upward into the branches of the towering oak, and know that it grew because it grew slowly and well. Slow me down, Lord, and inspire me to send my roots deep into the soil of life's enduring values, that I may grow toward the stars of your rewards. Amen.

Additional Scripture references for this chapter.

The promises of God	Psalm 27:14 KJV
	Psalm 34:15-22 KJV
	Psalm 37:3,4 KJV
	2 Corinthians 7:5,6 TLB
	Colossians 2:6 TLB
Our minds	Psalm 51:10 KJV
	Proverbs 12:5 KJV
	1 Corinthians 2:16 KJV, TLB
	1 Corinthians 3:20-23 TLB
	Romans 12:2 Amp.
God's Timing	Ecclesiastes 3:11 KJV

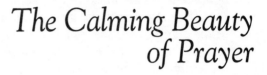

FIVE

The Calming Beauty of Prayer

I remember fantasizing about how wonderful it would be to have grandchildren. (Of course, forget the fact that Rick and Laurie were still teen-agers.) I imagined how dear it would be to be a grandmother.

As I've reflected on those fantasies, I've realized that the desire to be a grandmother was instilled in me by my mother, who was incredible as a grandma to my children.

Grandma Miller had everything going for her all the time. She'd arrive at our house with a bag of "stuff." Sometimes it was a fun T-shirt for Rick or a playsuit for Laurie. Other times it was one stick of gum. "Saved, just for *you*," she would lovingly explain.

But the relationship I loved observing most was the way my mother created a secret, a surprise, or an adventure with Laurie and Rick.

Mother always talked to me, but she whispered to my children. They had all sorts of highly personal conversations. The children talked over everything from how they got that big scratch on his or her leg to what great thing they'd seen in the park that day. All was confidentially shared with Grandma.

She taught them a thousand things in her short time with them, but I'm most grateful for her thorough, but brief, lessons on prayer. She made praying as easy as breathing for my children and for the children she taught at Sunday School, Daily Vacation Bible School, and after school Christian Release Time. And though Laurie was a preschooler at the time, it didn't matter. They prayed. "No fuss, no muss, just talk to the Lord about it," was her attitude.

After Mother died, I found her personal definition of prayer in one of her notebooks. It read,

> Personal prayer, it seems to me, is a simple necessity of life. It's as basic to an individual as sunshine, food, and water—and at times of course, much more so!
>
> Personal prayer, I believe, is our effort to get in touch with the infinite God. Oh, I know my prayers are imperfect. Of course they are, but then I'm an imperfect human being. (But God knows *that* already.)
>
> A thousand experiences have convinced me, beyond a shadow of a doubt, that prayer multiplies the strength of an individual and brings within the scope of his capabilities almost any conceivable objective!

Time and time again, I'd see Laurie or Rick up on her lap and hear them pouring out some trouble to her. If I strained my ears, I'd usually hear Mother responding by praying something like, "Now, Jesus, You know all about Billy down the street, and You know how he throws rocks. Please help Billy to stop doing that, and help Laurie to show Billy how to play and have fun. Amen." Then she'd add some words about, "Maybe Billy doesn't like his house, or his red hair or something. Maybe he needs love."

Grandmother and child would spend time together discussing the seriousness of the situation, and Jesus was always in on everything.

After she had these sessions with our children, I would be utterly stunned at the calming beauty of her prayers with them.

The woman, the teen-ager, or the child that can slip easily into prayer has a beauty formula going for her that no cosmetic on the market can beat.

It seems strange to me that, in spite of all the great books we read on prayer, we still miss its exciting importance in our lives.

Prayer is a fascinating spiritual voyage of discovery. Explorers in the realm of prayer are a little like Columbus when he landed on a new continent. In blind faith he had begged support from Queen Isabella for his adventure. He sailed unknown seas, and found a new land without having any idea of what opportunities lay beyond.

We probably have only just reached the edge of the beach in prayer. A vast, unknown continent lays out there beyond us, waiting to be explored, conquered, and cultivated. Nothing can be so thrilling as discovery, but some of us are so comfortable in our prayer rut that the mere thought of exploring tires us out completely.

Beautiful is the woman who joins in the highest of all discovery by adventuring into prayer. Just think, we don't need to leave home, work, or career. We don't need to stop any task we might be doing to carry on this adventure, because we carry God's mind in ours! We are with God every second, and He is with us.

Some women make an issue out of the verse, "Pray without ceasing" (1 Thessalonians 5:17 KJV).

"How can that possibly be?" they question. "Does that mean we are to stop everything, fold our hands, close our eyes, and stay that way all day?"

Absolutely not! There can be one or more times during the day when we give God our undivided attention. Then He can speak to us, and we can clearly hear Him. But just as our minds and souls are with us all the time, so is the Lord! Praying is as easy and effortless as breathing. God is here and ahead of us. If we stand still, He stands. If we move, He has already moved ahead, and we begin to know the joy of walking in His direction.

Over and over again, I've been asked if God really speaks to me, and if He does, how does He do it? It's not such a big mystery. Haven't you been grocery shopping or ironing and had a thought about a friend fly through your mind? It's someone you haven't thought of in months, so you start wondering how they are. Next, the thought that you should call, write, or go see them whizzes across your thinking. So, after a bit, you stop what you are doing and call them. After your hello, you may hear, "Oh, I've been hoping you would call; I really need you. I'm so grateful you called!"

My minister friend, Keith, has told me of many incidents of driving along the street and the thought (definitely from the Lord) would occur that he should turn at the next street and visit the Smiths or the Browns who live there. He's turned up the street, stopped at the house, rung the doorbell, and quietly listened as Mrs. Smith or Mrs. Brown says, "Oh, thank God, you've come! Please come in. We need you. We were just talking about you and we were wishing you were here."

Another friend, Bo Knowlton, told me that she was sewing up the seams in her new drapes when the name of her oldest son "popped" into her mind. Since she had a fearful feeling about him, she stopped sewing and breathed, "Lord, I know Dan is in Your hands, but I don't understand these terrible feelings. Please take care of him; he's Yours."

She went back to sewing; yet she continued mentally to hold Dan before the Lord. The bad vibrations grew stronger all afternoon, so she called a friend and, while admitting that everything was probably just fine with Dan, they prayed anyway and asked especially for the Lord to keep him safe.

Much later, when Dan was supposed to be home for dinner, she got a phone call from him. He was in a hospital and had been slightly hurt. All the players of his basketball team were on their way to a game in a neighboring city when the bus went off the road on a sharp curve, and, only by a miracle, it came to a stop just on the edge of a high precipice. There were no serious injuries, and Dan was just checking with his mom to tell her he was all right.

God speaks to us by the Holy Spirit's gentle voice in our minds. If that Spirit is unhindered, the voice of God can be remarkably clear.

If you haven't heard the Lord speaking directly to you, the key might be to examine what in your life may have silenced the Holy Spirit. I say *may* have silenced Him because it is not my intention to lay *any* guilt trips on anyone.

There are a few hindrances in our prayer lives that can bring what could be an adventurous experience down to an apathetic journey into boredom. Let me list three of the most common hindrances:

1. *We have not opened our lives completely to Christ.*

You may be like the woman in the hospital with my mother, who had prayed many prayers but all without faith, without Jesus, and without God's forgiveness. You must be born again and become as a child before you have access to God the Father.

Speaking to God is a little like speaking to the president of the United States. Because I have seen many pictures of our president, I would know him if I saw him in person. Because I have heard him over the air, I would recognize his voice if he spoke to me. If he ever invited me to dinner in the White House, I'd be able to say, "I've talked with the president." I'd know his thinking on some matters and his wishes and desires concerning certain issues and policies.

But, there is no way that I could have access to him, to his thinking, or to his help, like his children do! They are privileged. They have immediate access. They have priority. They are his family and they are loved. They can talk freely with the president, because he is their father.

We have to be God's children. It is not enough just to know what He is like, or in an emergency to "hear" His voice, or use His Word like a rabbit's foot for luck.

And, the only way to become God's child, to be born into His family, is to receive Jesus Christ as personal Savior. "But as many as received Him, to them gave He power to become the sons of God, even to them that believe on His name" (John 1:12 KJV).

2.   *We are harboring a long-time bitterness.*

It doesn't seem to matter how little or how big one's bitterness is, but rather that it is there. You may cherish a small resentment against your parents because they never took you to a dentist to have your teeth straightened. You may be bitter over a mother who, early in life, convinced you that you were artless and totally uncreative. Your father might have been an absentee father who always had time for business associates (or people in his congregation, as ministers are prone to do) but never shared any of himself with you.

You might be holding on to bitterness because of a loved one's death or your own debilitating lingering illness. Whatever its cause, bitterness will hopelessly clog the prayer channels to God. Known sin also separates one from God, and even though you may be a Christian, the Lord will not hear your prayers.

John 15:7 says, "But if you stay in Me and obey My commands, you may ask any request you like, and it will be granted!"

3.   *We aren't specific in our prayers.*

James knew about this lack of specifics when he wrote, "Ye have not because ye ask not" (James 4:2 KJV). Besides that, it's easier to be concerned for the "whole world of lost pagans" than the man we work for or the woman who checks our groceries at the store. When we generalize our prayers, it takes out the risk of our direct involvement. We don't have to chance an adverse reaction from distant heathen, but we do take risks when we relate to a neighbor. It costs nothing to love the nameless lost, but it costs everything to love the individuals we live with and know.

These are only a few of the reasons we may not have prayer's quiet, calming beauty evident in our lives.

The woman who has truly asked Christ to come into her life can have a wise, sane, yet wildly exciting prayer life. Here are some suggestions to help you achieve a beautiful prayer time.

1.   *Examine your thoughts and take a few deep breaths.*

Start with a house cleaning of your mental faculties. David talked about his time of "meditation". Take time to breathe deeply three or four times. It tends to relax us and to clear out the rubble of our minds. See what thoughts need to be thrown out of the closets of your mind. The bitter memories, the resentful attitudes toward others, and the grudges you have long harbored need to be banished. It may mean going to someone to ask forgiveness ... or to someone else to offer forgiveness.

James tells us, "Admit your faults to one another and pray for each other so that you may be healed. The earnest prayer of a righteous man has great power and wonderful results" (James 5:16).

Or, in your particular case, it may mean breaking the habit of showing your resentment toward someone by always being critical of them.

Read the entire passage in Colossians 3:12-15, but pay particular attention to the middle part where Paul says, "Be gentle and ready to forgive; never hold grudges. Remember, the Lord forgave you, so you must forgive others."

Paul talks about "making allowances for each other's faults because of your love" (see Ephesians 4:2.). So, clean out the grudges and memories and start with a fresh mind.

2. *Be wise in prayer.*

My pastor of many years, Dr. Edward Cole, told a story about a little girl who was asked what she would pray for if she were completely blind. She thought a moment and then answered, "I'd ask God for a dog with a collar and a chain to lead me around."

We pray a good many prayers like that—asking for a dog and a chain when we could ask for opened eyes. We are a bit foolish in the way we pray repetitious prayers or ask for such petty things.

We can be wise in praying if we remember that prayer is a two-way thing. God is here! He is with us by the power of the Holy Spirit. We have this delightful, hope-filled promise in Romans 8:26,27: "The Holy Spirit helps us with our daily problems and in our praying. For we don't even know what we should pray for, nor how to pray as we should; but the Holy Spirit prays for us with such feeling that it cannot be expressed in words. And the Father who knows all hearts knows, of course, what the Spirit is saying as He pleads for us in harmony with God's own will."

See? He made us and He knows us. He has not left us alone to fumble helplessly for words or to grapple feebly after God's miraculous power. The Holy Spirit even prays *for* us. Fantastic!

   3.   *Make a prayer list.*

Many authorities are suggesting the practical and therapeutic use of lists. Dr. Joyce Brothers has a whole book on making lists.

Here are some points that can be made in regard to our praying. A prayer list:

   a.   Helps you to be specific and remember your important needs.

   b.   Helps you to see what percentage of your prayers is for physical or material needs, and what percentage is for spiritual needs. It helps you see what the main priorities really are.

   c.   Helps you keep records so you avoid the rut of habit-prayed prayers. It also keeps track of personal miracles.

Since most of our daily lives seem to move non-stop at jet speed, lists are a valuable tool for keeping up with things. Otherwise, what we were desperately praying over two weeks ago may seem nothing compared to today's frantic concerns. In fact, to be truthful, we can't remember exactly what it was two weeks ago that took all our prayer time. But if we've kept a notebook and listed the requests, we can readily see God's hand at work.

My little notebooks are the twenty-nine cent variety. Put the name of the month at the top, write your requests down the left side, and mark off room down the right to fill in answers.

Remember the story of the people who gathered at the church to pray for much needed rain? Only one brought an umbrella. When you make a list of requests, leave room for a list of answers. God's Word says that if you pray in faith believing, He will answer.

I still have almost all of my old notebooks (going back

to 1959) and I find re-reading them a wonderful shot in the arm of my spirituality. Those notebooks are a record of God's incredible faithfulness to me. They chronicle God's hand, His intervention, His "yes"es and His "no"s, and His interesting timing—and on each page I breathe the words in Psalm 116:7, "Be at rest, once more, O my soul, for the Lord has been good to you" (New International Version).

Cover your list with your hand after you have prayed over each entry, and then thank God for working out each problem, for giving each answer, and for showing His loving will in each circumstance. God can be trusted.

He is the same yesterday, today, and tomorrow, and your list will be just one more proof to encourage you. (See Hebrews 13:8 KJV.)

4. *Try praying with someone.*

A familiar verse in Matthew states that where two or three are gathered in Christ's name, He is in the midst of them. But it's the verse just before that one that always gets to me. Jesus says, "I also tell you this—if two of you agree down here on earth concerning anything you ask for, my Father in Heaven will do it for you" (Matthew 18:19).

When my children were still at home, we prayed individually in our bedrooms and collectively at meal time, but I also prayed for each member of the family as they were dashing off for work or school. It daily demonstrated the truth that prayer could quench the spirit of hate, fear, and panic, when nothing else will even come close.

I had a quick prayer with Laurie and Rick. (They were always running a little late.) It's surprising how much I learned about their inner feelings and conflicts by asking them what I should pray about on any given morning. Once, before I could ask, Rick anticipated the question, and said, "Ten o'clock. Zoology class. Test."

Also, I'm sure a woman in Pomona High School's attendance office had no idea that one of her helpers (Laurie) prayed for her each morning. That didn't come easily for Laurie because she and this woman were not fond of each other. On the day I asked the Lord to give Laurie the ability to smile when she was working with her, Laurie dryly observed, "There you go, Mom, expecting miracles again!"

It was Dr. Ralph Byron, surgeon at City of Hope hospital in Duarte, California, who gave me the greatest clue to a couple praying together. He said to find the best time to pray (morning, night, or whenever) and then suggested the idea of the husband or wife leading on alternate days. One day the wife introduces a sentence prayer on request number one. Then the husband prays about that subject. Then the wife introduces request number two and the husband prays, and so on. He prays short, to-the-point prayers on as many subjects as the wife wants to bring up. The next time, the husband does the introducing and the wife prays. This kind of praying can bring a couple very close to the Lord and to each other.

You may not have a husband to pray with. You may have a non-Christian husband, who won't pray with you. You may have a Christian husband who is unwilling to join you in prayer. Don't let any of these hinder you from finding someone with whom to share this exciting prayer discovery. Modify it to suit your life, but by all means, *try* it. Who knows? Maybe there's someone, right now, in your life who would give anything to have a regular prayer session with you.

We can also pray while we sit in church. I firmly believe that if every person in the congregation prayed intensely while the pastor preached, we'd see miracle after miracle happen. If our churches are dying spiritually, it may not be the fault of the pastor or of the Lord. Maybe it because we are neglecting to pray.

The Holy Spirit is always eager to break through to us, and He finds an open door where Christians lovingly, joyously unite in prayer.

5. *Discover the joy of praying for someone else.*

When we were little children, our prayers tended to be simple, happy demands on Jesus. Children ask for small favors like a new teddy bear or healing for a cut knee. But as we began to mature both physically and spiritually, we began to pray in a different vein. We prayed in behalf of our families, loved ones, and neighbors. Then, after we've really begun to catch the magnitude of miracles that a prayer life can bring, we find we can even pray for strangers: the man on the curb waiting for the light to change, the lady in front of us at the post office, the truck driver behind us on the highway. They become fascinating subjects to talk over with the Lord.

Secret prayer for others, all during the day, is the acid test of our unselfishness. Self must fade out to clear a channel through which God's warmth can flow unhindered in lovely, unending prayer. To me, it seems, the highest form of communication is not asking God for things for ourselves, but letting Him flow through us, out, and over the world to others.

You might find, as I have, that when you are praying for a friend, the friend may be completely closed toward God, yet open to you. By praying for this friend, you can open her toward God. In a diagram, it looks like this.

           God hears, and then

I pray;   He helps
                                      my friend.

Because of my prayer, God speaks to my friend and the friend feels the first faint desire for God and slowly opens toward Him. Up to this point, there has been a wall between my friend and God, but then comes the connecting arrow of prayer and my friend is reached.

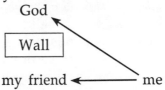

Prayer crumbles the wall.

God
↕
my friend

In another manner of speaking, if you help turn a friend toward God by prayer, you perform the same service as a telephone operator. You connect the friend with God. That helps God to speak directly, person-to-person, with that friend. (How beautiful the ways of prayer.)

At the beginning of this chapter, I shared some of the prayer concepts of my mother, whose prayer life was quite astonishing. I'd like to include one more "happening," for it involves this last point of praying for others.

On the day doctors discovered the first lumps on one breast, my mother's appointment was in the morning. By evening, she was in the hospital. Surgery was performed the next morning, the breast removed, and the whole thing was over incredibly fast.

I thought she probably didn't have time to jot down a note to me, as she always did before vacation trips or hospital visits, so I didn't expect one. But three years after the surgery, she died, and tucked away in one of her notebooks I found *the* note. It was not written to me, which explains why I never got it. Instead, it was a prayer she had penned the morning of that first doctor's appointment, after reading her morning devotions. At the top of the page is the Scripture reference, Romans 12:1. The passage deals with sacrifice or giving one's whole body to the Lord. Just under the reference she wrote,

> *Hand it over to the Lord for Him to live in it—the life that He pleases. Lord, You may do with me what You please. You may take this body and do with it as you desire. It is your body. I now present it to Thee and it's Yours from this moment on . . . Help Yourself to it.*

> *Lord, I'm going in the hospital. I'm just a weak, unknown handmaiden of Thine—with no knowledge of what's ahead or of the acquaintance with hungry hearts I may meet there.*

> *Here is my body—my hands, feet and lips. Take them and use them for some troubled, burdened hearts. Speak through my lips, Thy words of light and life.*

> *How wonderful to know that God is mine, to feel that He dwells in my heart, rules my will, my affections, my desires, and to know that He loves me!*   *Amen.*

I was astonished to find there was not one word, one line, or one mention of the surgery—nothing about the impending mastectomy or the possible diagnosis of cancer! Her only concern was for a needy stranger she might meet while hospitalized.

God answered that prayer faster than any other prayer she ever prayed. The first night after surgery she could not sleep, even though she had taken the pre-scribed sleeping pills. They simply did not take effect.

She lay there, in the wee hours of the morning, not in any particular pain, but curious as to why she was awake.

A nurse flicked her flashlight over Mother's face and said, "Why, Mrs. Miller, why are you awake at this hour?"

"Oh, I don't know, maybe I'm just awake so I can talk to you," she said.

Hearing that response, the nurse just flew out of the room without a word. Mother sensed there was something very wrong, so she began praying for the nurse.

A few hours later, the nurse returned to my mother's room. Mother asked her why she had left so suddenly and why she was so upset. For the next two hours, the nurse poured out the tragic events of that night and all that led up to it. Her marriage was all but over. Everything was wrong and out of control in her life.

After she had seen my mother the first time that night, she'd received permission to go home for a few hours to try to pull herself together. The nurse described in detail her feelings as she entered her house. She explained that she casually wondered what her friend's sweater and dress were doing on the couch, but she dismissed the thought as she went through the hall to the bedroom.

What she saw there exploded in her brain as a shocking, unbelievable bolt of lightening, and it instantly triggered a furious rage within her. Her best friend and her husband were together in bed, clutching each other as she yelled and screamed her fury at them. The nurse told my mother that she wanted to kill them but she had no gun, so she ran out of the house, got into the car, and drove around in a daze.

Finally, she decided what she must do. She went back to the hospital, intending to give herself a lethal injection of a drug that would end her life. She started down the hall, but as she came to my mother's room, something compelled her to look in.

Now as she stood before Mother a second time, though she was crying and shaking violently, she asked, "Mrs. Miller, when I was here earlier, why did you say you were awake to talk to me?"

Mother replied that God had not let her sleep and since she'd seen no one else, she figured it was the nurse who needed the Lord. So, Mother explained that she was probably awake so she could pray for her, and she had— all night.

In spite of the fact that my mother had been out of surgery less than twenty-four hours, she led the young woman to the healing hands of Jesus, the Great Physician. The young nurse prayed, received Christ as her Savior, and put her trust in God. The two women talked until the morning nurse arrived for duty.

For the rest of my mother's hospitalization, she counseled and prayed with the young nurse who had accepted Christ. Mother had the joy of watching as the Lord picked up the pieces of the girl's shattered soul and replaced the fragments with a brand new heart.

I wonder what miracles of beauty could be wrought in our lives and in those around us if we daily experienced the calming beauty of prayer?

Additional Scripture references for this chapter.

Reasons for unanswered prayer	Psalm 66:18,20 TLB - secret sin
	Proverbs 1:24-32 TLB - indifference
	Proverbs 21:13 TLB - neglect of mercy
	Proverbs 28:9 TLB - despising the law

Isaiah 59:1-2 TLB - sin
James 1:6-8 TLB - instability
James 4:3 TLB, KJV -
  self indulgence

*Conditions of
answered prayers*

2 Chronicles 7:14 KJV -
  forgiveness
Jeremiah 29:13 RSV -
  seek wholeheartedly
Mark 11:24 KJV - faith
1 John 3:22 TLB -
  asking in His will
1 John 5:14 TLB -
  asking in His will

God hears!

Psalm 4:3-5 TLB
Psalm 18:6 KJV
Psalm 34:17 TLB
Psalm 91:15-16 TLB
Proverbs 15:29 TLB
1 Peter 5:7 TLB

SIX

Inferiority: The Green-Eyed Cat

"What would you change about women in general (if you could wave some sort of magic wand)?" I began research for this book by asking various people that question. Here are some of the responses, and for the purpose of clarification, I've included a bit about who gave them.

1. "I'd like for women to be more feminine" (a man married to a very, rigid, structured woman).

2. I'd like to put kindness into women's voices" (my son, Rick, the box boy who had just gotten off work at the grocery store and was tired of cranky female checkers).

3. "I'd like for women to fix up their outward looks and lose weight" (a young man married two years to a girl who seems to need exactly that).

4. "I'd like for women to stop being so petty about situations that involve co-workers" (an exasperated bank vice-president, who had spent several hours resolving a dispute between two women employees over a 10-minute discrepancy in lunch schedules).

5. I'd like to open women's eyes to the world around them" (the owner of a modeling and charm school, who also mentioned that some women's thought processes were about as deep as a "Texas mud puddle").

6. "I'd like for girls to stop knocking themselves" (a young, unmarried, male checker at my grocery store. He'd just had a date with a "really beautiful" girl who was "well built," and each time he told her how great she looked, she had *denied* it).

7. "I'd like for women to be outspoken and talk more" (This one really puzzled me until I realized this man is married to an absolutely gorgeous angel who has a quiet, gentle nature. He doesn't know what he's got!).

8. "I'd like for women to be less critical" (a young woman who had just returned from two hours at a baby shower).

9. "I'd like for women to quit trying to impress their bosses and just be themselves" (a principal of a school which employs fifteen women teachers).

10. "I wish women would stop saying, 'I'm *just* a housewife,' in the same tone of voice they use to describe common constipation" (me, because I believe there is no such thing as "just a housewife").

I asked many more people this question, and, while the answers varied according to their lifestyle or marital status, one common thread ran through all of the answers. In one way or another, directly or indirectly, they wanted us as women to get rid of our low estimate of ourselves.

Nothing will wreck my ability to be a successful woman of God, to be a creative person, or to get along with others more than the feeling that I have little or no value. Accepting myself is one of the main hinges on the door to accepting others. What I think of myself influences all my actions and responses toward others.

A woman I met recently told me about her job as a social worker with children. She said that she often began her session with children by asking them to tell her, or to write on paper, two or three things that they liked about themselves. Usually the children couldn't think of one single positive thing. But, when she asked them to tell or write about the things they *disliked* about themselves, they had no problem, instantly telling or writing their long list of faults.

Today I asked myself to name two things about myself that I liked, and only because I knew the question beforehand did I answer with something. I find I'm like the children the social worker deals with; I find good qualities are hard to admit and bad qualities seem to run rampant and are easily spotted. Perhaps we all need to discover the origins of our low self esteem; look at the problems they create in our lives; examine what they eventually produce in our personalities; and recognize how low self esteem controls our responses and actions to others.

1. *I believe that a sense of worthlessness is rooted in our past.*

When did our low opinion of ourselves begin? Probably when we were babies. Incredible as that sounds, think about it.

It's so easy when we're shopping in the grocery store and we pass a couple holding a baby in one of those infant-seat carriers. If the baby is cute, pretty, or absolutely darling, we find ourselves talking, cooing, and verbally showering it with love and acceptance. "Oh, my, what a darling! What a sweetie-pie you are." We go on and on because we just *love* babies . . . or do we?

Not five minutes later, in the parking lot, another woman holding her baby walks toward us. Once more we get all enthused about babies ... until we see the baby. His head may be slightly enlarged, or is covered with unruly or dirty hair. His look is not alert but dull, and his face may be misshapen and homely. We quickly turn the other way. We say *nothing at all*. Our silence condemns the baby.

I feel almost certain that the infant in the parking lot knows he's been rejected. He is learning from our mere vibrations that there is something not quite acceptable about him. He is already experiencing the first painful feelings of insecurity.

Look at your life for a moment, and think back with me. What were you teased about in your early life at home or in school? Was it your red hair or freckles, your buck teeth or oversized nose, your fatness or your skinniness, your protruding ears or the space between your two front teeth, or was it your lisping or stuttering problem? Perhaps it was even your name, but whatever it was, very few of us have escaped the cutting wounds of childhood remarks.

Remember the saying many of us were taught when we were in grade school?

"Sticks and stones may break my bones, but names will never hurt me."

I'm not sure who made that up, but it probably was designed to help take the sting out of our wounds when someone called us names that were painful. Closer, much closer, to the truth are these lines I heard the other day.

"Sticks and stones may break my bones, but names do permanent damage."

The teasing that hurt my feelings the most was always about my being thin. I think I know every joke about thin people that has ever been devised or uttered. I wish I had a nickel for all the times I was called "bird legs" or referred to as "skinny as a pole." The advice to "put a little meat on your bones" was given to me often during those days.

I was physically more than a little late in maturing, and in our worship-the-bosom culture, I found gym classes particularly disturbing. I had rheumatic fever when I was ten and never took regular physical education classes after that. I had "rest" instead. Why I had to suit up, and how I managed always to be assigned a locker next to a girl who was "really built", I'll never understand! (I won't even go into the matter of taking those awful see-all-of-everybody gym showers!)

School is not the only place our personhood is whittle down; home life can be just as destructive. Our families— unknowingly or deliberately—can contribute a great deal to our feelings of worthlessness.

For instance, if some one tells us often enough that we are clumsy, dumb, or even in the way, we become quite good at being clumsy, dumb, or in the way. Or, if we as parents allow our kids to destructively criticize each other ... then they will. That's not limited to kids, however. Adults have also been known to judge each other often as well.

Just recently I was watching a documentary on some very effective classroom teaching techniques, and one of the children was asked why he thought everyone was learning so much in this class and why everyone was having fun, yet learning. The little eight- or nine-year-old boy said instantly, "Well, in the beginning, our teacher told us there was only one rule for her class. *"Nobody can insult anybody else."*

"Is that a good rule?" asked the interviewer.

"Oh yes," came the answer. "It means that whatever I say or how I look ... no one can laugh at me or call me stupid."

Interesting rule. So, I looked up the word insult in my dictionary and found it to mean (1) an attack and (2) any act or speech meant to hurt the feelings or self respect of another.

If an insult is an "act or speech" meant to wound someone, then it seems to me that the classroom rule, "Nobody can insult anybody else," is a hallmark rule and one that needs to be practiced at home first, in the outside world and wherever two people are together.

Our silent *acts* of rejection or disapproval and our verbal beatings on one another are lifelong insults that live forever in our emotions and minds.

I know the truth of this because I meet many grown women who are still handicapped by some action or word of people in their past. One young wife tearfully recounted her twelfth Christmas. Her mother took a temporary job to buy presents. However, after twenty years, the mother was still at that "temporary" job. "We did get a lot of nice presents," the woman said, "but while my mother was away so much of the time my sister was lost to the world of drugs."

Many adults cannot remember their mothers or fathers hugging them, kissing them, or ever saying, "I love you."

A mother of four children recalled that her mother repeatedly told her, "You can't do *anything* right!" Then, this young woman added, "Since I can't get along with *my* four kids, I guess my mother was right."

Another young woman has a hard time relating to the opposite sex because all she knows about men is that her father spent his every waking moment yelling at her for something. A woman in her forties has great difficulty being intimate with her husband. During counseling she learns it's because of earlier abuses by her father.

One woman remembers being introduced as a child by a tactless, thoughtless mother who said, "This is Jane, our little red-headed monster."

I am not qualified or capable to begin to assess the damage that has been inflicted on these women. I am not prepared to comment on the colossal ignorance of any parent who would yoke a child with all kinds of painful burdens, but I do believe that as a mother and a parent, I stand before God and must answer to Him for all charges of parental irresponsibility. If I had the power—and I don't—I think I'd make the "no insults" rule into a law. Of course, one could never legislate, much less enforce, such a law, but maybe it would be a deterrent to "acts and speech" which crush the soul.

As we move on into adulthood, we take the insecurities from our past with us. We have our ups and downs, but some of us are down too often and for incredibly long periods of time. We wonder why.

2.   *Lack of a sense of worth is depression's basic requirement.*

Here is part of the answer. Located at the very source of our down period is the lack of self-esteem. We all suffer from it, to one degree or another.

I find depression in people everywhere. There are many different levels of depression, from a casual "I've got the blahs," to the deadly calm of a person teetering on the edge of suicide. It comes in all ages, and one unbelievable time I saw it in a baby.

When I finished a speaking engagement for the U. S. Army overseas, I was asked to go to the back of the auditorium to meet a young couple. Before I was halfway down the aisle, I spotted the two obviously sad and very stressed-out people and their baby.

It seemed the couple had been profoundly moved (and more than a little upset) by what I had shared relative to relationships in marriage. They had identified completely with the factors that tear apart marriage and had experienced some of the same sins, anger, and rebellion in their lives that I had in mine. They listened as I told how God could move in our lives, but they could not or would not bring themselves to trust the Lord. As I talked with them, they seemed very angry at each other and at the world in general, and I sensed they were both deeply depressed. What hit me hardest was the realization that nowhere was their own emotional depression more clearly reflected than in the face of their ten-month-old son.

The baby sat quietly enough on his father's lap, but all his parents' inner ugliness and dissatisfaction was clearly written on his little face.

Because they had identified so closely with my story, the air between us was charged with a bit of emotional tension. To give some relief to the moment, I reached over, touched the baby's cheek, and said, "Hi, Sweetie." He was very solemn and I couldn't coax a smile or anything close. His face was so troubled and homely that it made my heart ache. In order to bridge the awkwardness of the moment and to swallow the lump in my throat, I tried to make conversation. Looking at his mother and as cheerfully as possible, I asked, "What's the baby's name?" She never looked up at me. The father said, in the most degrading tone of voice, "His name is Boy." (I thought the name of Boy was only used in old Tarzan movies.)

"Boy?" I asked. I still couldn't believe anyone would give their son that name.

"Yes, Boy," he repeated. That's *all* he is . . . Boy," the father spoke in a clipped, disgusted, impatient way. The baby sat still and regarded me with his dull, almost unseeing eyes.

In the June 1990 issue of Better Homes and Gardens, in an article entitled *Stopping Childhood Depression in It's*

Tracks, the question was asked, "Do babies get blue or depressed?" The answer quoted from University of Miami Professor Tiffany Field PhD, was yes. "Most at risk," Dr. Field says, "are infants with depressed mothers. Usually you can tell at birth what the temperament of these kids is. They're poker faces; they won't imitate you or laugh at funny sounds."

While I'm not a doctor, I know that the little but precious human being called "Boy" was already depressed with his life, and because of his mother's and father's own degree of depression, Boy was a serious "most-at-risk" baby.

I wonder what effect the name "Boy" will have on him as he grows up? Will he be quiet and seemingly well behaved in school? Will his parents and teachers remember him as a "good" boy? And will they be unbelievably shocked when, at some later date, this young man's depression and feelings of worthlessness turn into an angry rage as he cries out to be heard by committing a horrendous act of violence? I wonder.

3.   *Lack of a sense of worth makes a woman's thoughts and speech suspicious, negative, and critical.*

The woman with little sense of personal worth sees her life and the world around her through darkly tinted glasses. Nothing is really good, and nothing turns out right for her. What's more, she is sure everyone else sees things out of the same dark glasses.

One such woman told me that every time she went to church people "talked bad" about her, and she was serious (boy, was she serious!).

"The minute I sit down they start whispering about me!" she said.

"What do they say?" I asked.

Her only answer was, "All lies, lies, lies!"

Because she had no self esteem, she was paranoid that

everywhere she went (especially church) people were against her, out to get her, and telling lies about her.

This kind of woman is so *sure* no one will like her (she doesn't like herself, so how *could* anyone else like her?) that when you walk up to her and say hello, she freezes like a popsicle right before your eyes.

When you speak to her, she's immediately suspicious of your motives and wonders why you are prying into her life by asking such personal questions. She's thinking "Why do you want to speak to me?". . . and "What did you mean by asking that?" She doesn't trust anyone or anything.

If she's on a vacation to Mexico, she's sure the bottled water is contaminated.

If she's at the best seafood restaurant on the waterfront, she complains about the "fishy smell in here."

If you ask her how her work is coming, be prepared for the worst possible report.

If you compliment her on her dress, she will tell you (1) how old it is (2) how much she paid for it, and (3) how she's always hated it.

If you tell her you like the way she's fixed her hair, she will tell you it needs a perm. Then she'll go on to tell you that her nose is too big or too long, or her face is too fat or too narrow. (The awful thing is that you never noticed before, but from now on, whenever you see her, those irregularities will probably be the *only* things you will see.)

If she wants you to come over to her house for dinner, she never invites you straight on. She says, "You wouldn't want to come over for dinner, would you?"

In the first chapter of *Ms Means Myself*, Gladys Hunt talks about women like this one I've just described— women who are all hemmed in by their lack of a sense of worth.

. . . some women are like tightly closed buds, atrophying on the vine. Afraid to open up, they do not dare risk the bloom lest it be less beautiful than someone else's.

Others become harping critics, quick to point out error in someone else and slow to love. Others don't criticize, they just internalize, never letting anyone know who they really are. They don't risk exposure or love or acceptance. Some play games, wearing the mask of a role they have chosen, sometimes a very spiritual role. Those are outwardly pious and inwardly barren, still unknown to anyone else or themselves. Others talk too much, skirting all the issues which might reveal their real person. And still others become authorities on any subject, even Bible quotes, to hide blatant insecurities.[1]

If we are negative, critical women, it's our tongues that give us away. The tongue reflects all the inner workings of the heart.

"The boneless tongue, so small and weak,
      can crush and kill," declares the Greek.
"The tongue destroys a greater horde,"
      the Turk asserts, "than does the sword."
"The tongue can speak a word whose speed,"
      says the Chinese, "outstrips the steed."
While Arab sages this impart;
      "The tongue's great storehouse is the heart."
From Hebrew wit and maxim sprung,
      "Though feet may slip, ne'er let the tongue."
The sacred writer crowns the whole,
      "Who keeps his tongue, doth keep his soul."
                              (writer unknown)

---

[1] Zondervan Publishing House, Grand Rapids, Michigan.

The tongue is not the only problem. Something else is deeply effected by our insecurities.

4.   *Lack of a sense of worth changes the pitch and intonation of the voice.*

A good actor is one who can "pretend" to be a character and speak his or her lines. A *great* actor is one who can *"be"* the character and by vocal expressions *"live"* his or her spoken lines. The actor's voice inflection makes the character believable or unbelievable.

In everyday life, we cannot pretend and merely speak polite lines. Whatever is missing inside will come out one way or another. The quickest is by mouth.

Somehow, almost mysteriously, when a woman is sure she is nothing or is "just a housewife," something happens to her vocal chords. Everything that's uttered from the larynx seems to be pre-set on a whining, pitying, and nagging pitch.

It's a beautiful day. You dash into the choir room on Sunday morning, grab your robe and music, and say to a woman who has very little sense of self worth, "Good morning! How are you this gorgeous day?"

Her whole face sags as she sniffs and whimpers, "Oh, I've got the blahs, I guess."

Her whining tone is familiar; you remember hearing it in your children when they were age three. From then on, nothing you say to her cheers her up or turns her on to a more enthusiastic day. The conversation just sputters out of words and dies.

Matthew Henry said, "They who complain most are most to be complained of."

The woman in the choir room, who whined about her "blahs", awakened to the same beautiful day you and I did, but she let her sense of worthlessness overshadow and darken the entire morning. She is very uptight about the extra pounds she's gained around her waistline, and perhaps a family member made a crack about her weight. But it seems to be the summation of all her inner thoughts. "I'm fat." That's all she thinks of, so when you innocently ask "How are you", there is no way she can put away her insecurities and simply answer the question without giving herself away by the tone of her voice.

Madame Lola Montez, who lived in the eighteen hundreds, said,

> "One of the most powerful auxiliaries of beauty is a fine, well-trained voice. Indeed, one of the most fascinating women I ever knew had scarcely any other charm to recommend her. She was a young countess in Berlin, who had dull eyes, a rough skin, with dingy complexion, coarse dull hair, and a dumpy frame. But she had an exquisite voice, which charmed everybody who heard it (*The Arts and Secrets of Beauty* cited earlier).

If only all of us would reevaluate our true self-worth, accept our weight, our hair, and whatever else, perhaps others would notice that we've got marvelous songs to sing. This woman (from the choir) is so unhappy with herself that she continually looks for loopholes and flaws in others to soothe her feelings or worthlessness.

Nagging is also a by-product of a poor self-image. It almost always destroys the nagger and the nagged. The destructive quality of nagging reaches a long way and lingers a long time.

My brother, Cliff, had a male teacher in grammar school who spent two semesters nagging him. I don't know what insecurities were at the bottom of this teacher's remarks to Cliff. Perhaps the man could have been helped. But, what I do know is that he almost destroyed my brother by picking on him and nagging him.

Of all the thousands of words teachers spoke to Cliff, my brother remembers most clearly this teacher, his words, and his tone of voice. A year's nagging was summed up in these words spoken by the teacher, "Cliff, you're so dumb and stupid, you'll never make it through high school—much less college! Why don't you just drop out of school and watch 'Popeye' on TV?"

Those remarks killed off most of Cliff's incentive to learn, and only after many years (and some war experiences in Vietnam) did Cliff reestablish a better self-image and go back to his studies.

I'd love to tell Cliff's teacher that the "dumb and stupid" boy not only made it through high school, he received his master's degree, made the list of "Who's Who in Colleges," and presently is not too far off from earning his doctorate.

5.   *Lack of a sense of worth convinces women that the grass is greener on the other side of the fence and that everyone else has it made!*

We all have to cope with disillusionment and sometimes we find ourselves in a sober or bad mood. But according to Dr. Theodore I. Rubin, writing in the *Ladies Home Journal*, "Acute disillusionment generates more serious depression and self-hate, and can even lead to suicide. Disillusionment is never possible without fantasy."

Fantasy is no stranger to most of us, and early in childhood we begin to know we live in two worlds—the real and the imagined. Many times our fantasies become a way of handling our insecurities and problems. One woman said, "I used to spend hours aching, dreaming of the kind of mother I so wished I had."

When we permit ourselves to live in a fantasy world, we rob ourselves of the opportunity to see God at action in our real world. It becomes very difficult to separate the facts from fantasy, and then we *really* have problems.

Looking at and comparing the success of others, the beauty of others, the brains of others, and the wealth of others with our own can lead to the biggest fantasy of all. Feelings of low self-worth and jealousy join with the spirit of coveting to push us straight down the road toward Depressionville.

See how many of the following statements you've heard lately.

"I don't have any talents. Mrs. Jones just makes me sick because she's got so many!"

"That may work for Sue. She relates well to people, but I don't, so I won't accept the nomination."

"You should see the mansion Beverly just moved into. She's got more bathrooms than I've got rooms in my whole house."

"Naturally, if I looked as beautiful as Clare, I'd be radiant and charming too!"

"You don't know what it's like to try to live on a pension check each month. You're loaded with money."

"Well, if I was married to Harry, I'd be a terrific wife, too. I'd like to see her married to my George for six months. She'd never make it."

"You kids are driving me crazy. I've tried to be a good mother to you . . . why don't you act more like the Brown's kids?"

David knew all about this kind of wishful fantasizing. If you have *The Living Bible,* read the entire seventy-third Psalm. Here are just a few statements from that chapter to give you new insights on an old problem.

"For I was envious of the prosperity of the proud and wicked. Yes, all through life their road is smooth! They grow sleek and fat. They aren't always in trouble and plagued with problems like everyone else . . . These fat cats have everything their hearts could ever wish for!" (vv. 3-7).

It was Shakespeare who wrote in *Othello*, "O! Beware, my lord, of jealousy; it is the green-eyed monster which doth mock the meat it feeds on."

Later in the seventy-third Psalm, David decided to go to God's sanctuary and spend some time meditating about his jealous feelings. He concludes, "Their [evil men's] present life is only a dream!" (v. 20).

Still later he states, "I saw myself so stupid and so ignorant; I must seem like an animal to You, O God. But even so, You love me!" (vv. 22, 23).

I'll stop there, but the seventy-third Psalm goes on to a magnificent conclusion. I hope you'll finish it. Each time I read that chapter, I come away just breathless because of David's words to the Lord, "But even so, You love me."

Herein lies the key to overcoming the low self-esteem we all experience. It begins with realizing that God's love to us is unconditional!

The woman who picks and claws at the beauty or success of others is most ugly, and she is crippled by her feeling of worthlessness.

The woman who indulges in fantasies is living in an unrealistic, imaginary world. She misses the intoxicating joy of real living.

The woman of little self-worth who continually longs to have someone else's looks, husband, talent, or house is pathetically misusing her time here on earth. Her life is a monumental waste of effort and energy, particularly in view of what it could be. She slides deeper into the quicksand of depression and does not see the solid, outstretched hand of God. She bypasses all He has planned for her, and she completely misses His words when He says, "My dear child, grab hold of me, take my hand and

I'll pull you out. I'll set you free. You are very precious to me, and I have come to rescue you. Take my hand. Come unto me. I love you."

If you, like me, have identified in any way with the woman of low self-esteem, there's good news. We can change that. We can lift our level, upgrade our position, and raise our own sense of worth by starting here and now. Realize first that God is pouring out His love upon you right now—this very second. Reread Ephesians 1:4 in *The Living Bible*. It says "Long ago, even before he made the world, God chose us to be his very own, through what Christ would do for us; he decided then to make us holy in his eyes, without a single fault—we who stand before him covered with his love."

Start with the truth of these words—they're from the Lord—and then look into your mirror and begin to see yourself as God sees you . . . "without a single fault" and "covered with his love."

Additional Scripture references for this chapter.

David's look into his own mirror	Psalm 73 TLB
God's promise	Isaiah 40:28,31,32 TLB
God's gifts to us	1 Corinthians 2:11,12 TLB
The new me	2 Corinthians 2:11,12 TLB
God gives	2 Corinthians 5:17 TLB Hebrews 4:13-16 TLB

SEVEN

The Poised Beauty of Self-Acceptance

At a time when the Reverend David Ray was pastoring the Valley Community Church of San Dimas, California, he interviewed me for one of his television specials. He was talking about my booklet *To Lib or Not to Lib*, and we discussed some of the ways a woman becomes a whole person because of Christ.

Toward the end of the interview, Reverend Ray asked me to name some of the positive characteristics found in women and in womanhood today.

I felt a little overwhelmed because the interview was coming to a close, and it was hard to answer such complex questions so quickly.

I'm glad I don't have a time limit here so we can really look at a few of those characteristics in depth.

It seems to me there are three very basic attributes prevalent in a poised, beauty-filled, Christian woman. The three traits connect and interrelate to a woman's self-concept.

As I said in the previous chapter, it all begins with our realizing our worth in God's sight—not our's. If we have accepted ourselves as God has accepted us, that concept becomes the very pulse beat of our lives. It is the inner "thump, thump, thump" that says, "I'm alive, I'm alive, I'm alive!" God thought us so valuable that He laid down His life to reach us and to save us. If we really know this, our whole lives glow with this first trait.

1.   *A woman accepts God's forgiveness and His evaluation of her.*

Gladys Hunt feels so strongly about the problems of a low self-image that she writes:

> I am increasingly convinced that a major cause of the despondency, the ineffectual living, the lack of freedom, the feeling of worthlessness so common in today's world is a failure to understand what God has done in redeeming us—and how and why He has done it.

When a woman begins to understand that God has forgiven her and actually accepts His forgiveness, fantastic things can happen! She can escape the confining cocoon of a non-person and explode into the sunshine of person-hood as a whole person.

However, if a woman asks God to forgive her but then refuses (for one reason or another) to accept that forgiveness, a shroud of frustration can envelop her life. If she does not think of herself as a child of God, she lives out her existence in loneliness, like some poor forgotten orphan.

John said, "But to all who received Him, He gave the right to become children of God" (John 1:12).

Some women have never realized, capitalized on, or utilized the *right* to become God's children. I find that sad and completely unnecessary. John must have given it some thought too, because immediately he adds, "All they needed to do was trust Him to save them."

Some women tell me they can't accept God's forgiveness because their particular sins are too many or too big. Inwardly I smile because I always rush to the conclusion that God will change his mind about forgiving *that* sin of mine. We forget that God is not shocked by our sins because He already knows all about them!

As I said in a previous chapter, one of the most beautiful verses in the Word of God tells us that God, who knows all, loved us anyway. Let me repeat it here for you.

Long ago, even before He made the world, God chose us to be His very own, through what Christ would do for us; He decided then to make us holy in His eyes, without a single fault, we who stand before Him covered with His love (Ephesians 1:4).

The next time you hear someone say they can't believe or accept the fact that God has forgiven them, tell them this:

"Yes, it is true that when I stood before the Lord to ask His forgiveness,
My dress was ragged and tattered because of my ugly sins,
My hair was thickly tangled with the webs of my rebellion,
My shoes were torn and muddied by my past failures.

But God never saw any of that!

He saw me as holy,
And He saw me as perfect,
Because I was dressed in His righteousness,
And He has covered me with the full-length cape of His love,
He saw nothing else!

Even when I explained how I really looked
underneath, He heard and He forgot *forever*.
The dimension of His forgetfulness is as far as
the East is from the West,
And it endures past all of eternity!"

Peter also reveals our worth in God's sight when he
says, "Dear friends, God the Father chose you long ago
and knew you would be His children" (1 Peter 1:2 TLB).
Just think:
You have come from God.
You belong to God.
You are important to God.
You will return to God.
Fortunately for us, our God does not evaluate us by
society's standards. He does not hold up a beauty chart
and check off our measurements or compare our statistics.
He does not require us to take periodic I.Q. tests to reveal
our degree of intelligence. He does not examine our Dun
and Bradstreet credit report to see what we have accomplished financially. God is not hampered, in any way, by
this world's cockeyed value system. He sees us as already
perfect in Christ. It is a guilt- and condemnation-free value
system.

David makes this quite clear when he writes, "O God,
You have declared me perfect in Your eyes" (Psalm 4:1
TLB). This verse, just by itself, would be an important one
in accepting God's forgiveness, but there's a lot more to
it than that.

How could David have written in one place that God
had declared him perfect and written in another, "O Lord,
you have examined my heart and know everything about
me?" (Psalm 139:1).

My mind boggles a bit when I think of the total picture
the Scriptures have given us about David. If we are not

too familiar with David, we could think of him only in terms of the mighty warrior and slayer of Goliath, writer of the Psalms, and famous king of all Israel. However, the other side of his life, the human and very weak traits of his character tend to remind us of "All My Children" or "Knots Landing," or some other television soap opera. By our standards, David didn't even come close to winning "Best King of the Year" award some years.

If there was any person in all of history who had a right to feel more worthless than David, I can't imagine who it would be. Consider these sins and failures.

1. He committed adultery.
2. He committed murder.
3. He was highly joyous one day and deeply depressed the next.
4. Absalom, David's older son, murdered his brother.
5. David failed as a father.
6. David failed in communicating to his wives.

I'm so glad that the Bible gives us a clear picture of him. Otherwise, we might have said, "Look at David, the handsome, famous, talented king of Israel. No wonder he was so great. He had no problems, and no hang-ups."

God "knew everything" about him, yet declared him perfect!

After David admitted God's all-knowing power (in Psalm 139:1), he does a second thing; he thanks God for making him the way he is (see verse 14). That included thanking God for his disadvantages as well as for his talents and great characteristics.

Maybe we need to try thanking God for the handicaps in our lives: those disturbing childhood memories or that wart on your nose, or other physical imperfections. It is never easy, but it can be done when we remember that *God only sees us in our perfect state.* He sees the finished product of our lives; our "warts" never show up in His viewfinder.

Thank God for your life, because God's value system says you are beautiful! (I'll write more in depth on thanking God in a later chapter.)

Also, David has shot his arrow right on target by writing the four-letter word *will* over and over.

"O Lord I *will* praise you"

"I *will* bless the Lord"

"I *will* cry unto the Lord"

"I *will* abide"

"I *will* sing"

"I *will* trust"

David, knowing all the inner facets of his life, made his daily living a matter of his will. In view of his sins and failures, it makes sense to conjecture that David must not have *felt* like

praising,

blessing,

thanking,

singing, or

abiding on many of his days,

but he did not leave it up to how he felt. He experienced feelings, but he did not allow them to control his will. In short, he made up his mind! We always tend to underestimate the power of our minds.

Personally, I think women are more gifted in displaying and using will power than men. When a woman sets her mind to doing something, you can count on it being done. She has a fantastic gift for making up her mind if she wants to!

It was the great Henrietta Mears, who best caught the power of using our will and making up our minds when she stated:

Will is the whole man active. I cannot give up my will; I must exercise it. I must will to obey. When God gives a command or a vision of truth, it is never a question of what He will do, but what we will do. To be successful in God's work is to fall in line with His will and to do it His way. All that is pleasing to Him is a success.[1]

Think of a strong, vibrant, godly woman who is dying of breast cancer. We go to her to give comfort and we come away comforted. We reach out to help her and we receive blessings instead. Whenever this happens, you can be sure that somewhere along the line she has acknowledged *how she feels* at the moment of her deepest grief and then has *made up her mind* to accept her loss and say, "What do You want me to learn from this, Father?" We stand in awe of this woman; yet what she has done should be the norm, not the exception, for a Christ-centered woman.

My mother's notes revealed this humorous truism. "The Lord gave us two ends to use—one to sit with and one to think with. Our success depends on which end we use the most. Heads we win, tails we lose."

Another woman is still whipping herself for failures and sins she committed thirty-five years ago. She's simply not using her correct end! She forgets every present joy. The fact that God has given her one blessing after another completely escapes her. She has no sense of worth; she cannot take God's forgiveness; and she lets how she feels direct her entire life. The sad part is that after so many years of letting her guilt feelings, her sad feelings, her failure feelings, dictate her waking hours, she can no longer

---

[1] *Henrietta Mears and How She Did It!*, Ethel May Baldwin, Regal Books, Glendale, California 1966.

use her mind. She can't really make up her mind about anything. Even the simple task of deciding between having baked or mashed potatoes for dinner has become an enormous chore.

If this woman went to a psychiatrist or a psychologist, she could pay a great deal of money per hour to hear him say, almost word for word, what Paul said a long time ago, "Accept life, and be most patient and tolerant with one another, always ready to forgive if you have a difference with anyone" (Colossians 3:12 PH).

The doctor would probably tell her to accept her life, her past failures, and her unhappy childhood. He'd advise her of what her bitterness is doing to her. If he were a Christian doctor, he'd talk about forgiving God, forgiving others, forgiving herself, and forgiving circumstances. He'd try to get her to thank God even in these present moments, and he'd convince her to use her mind in a constructive way.

When we put our inferiority feelings away and make living, praising, and singing a matter of the will, we really awaken our sleepy, run-down minds. Don't be discouraged if your mind is slow to cooperate. Keep at it, because Paul says, "But strange as it seems, we Christians actually do have within us a portion of the very thoughts and mind of Christ!" (1 Corinthians 2:16).

It was Toki Miyashina who made this paraphrase of the twenty-third Psalm. Read it aloud, for it will help prepare you for achieving the first trait found in the poised beauty of self-acceptance.

The Lord is my pacesetter,
    I shall not rush;
He makes me stop and rest
    for quiet intervals.
He provides me with images of stillness
    which restore my serenity.

He leads me in ways of efficiency
    through calmness of mind
And His guidance is peace.
Even though I have a great many
    things to accomplish each day,
    I will not fret;
For His presence is here.
His timelessness, His all importance
    will keep me in balance.
He prepares refreshment and renewal
    in the midst of my activity.
By anointing my mind with His oils of tranquility
    my cup of joyous energy overflows.
Surely harmony and effectiveness
    shall be the fruits of my hours
For I shall walk in the pace of my Lord
    and dwell in His house forever.

The trait I've just discussed, of accepting God's forgiveness and His evaluation, has everything to do with our vertical relationship to God. This next trait goes out from us, horizontally, toward others. Sometimes our ability to reach out to others (or the degree of success involved) is sharply curtailed by our low self-estimate and our obsession with "My problem."

The woman who has accepted God's forgiveness in her life and has begun to thank Him for each and every aspect of her life should lose her critical tongue, and she will, if she glows with the next trait.

2.   *The woman has developed the no-knock policy in all relationships.*

It's been said that people who *feel* inferior *talk* about it. The most critical of all people, as I mentioned in the previous chapter, are the ones who have little or no feelings of value or worth. They are terribly preoccupied with "poor me" attitudes. Sometimes they are unaware of others in their own families who are bleeding and crying for help. Often they become extremely critical (vocally) toward everyone. They feel such a failure in what they are doing that they cannot accept someone else's success.

There is definitely something you can do to break the negative pattern of your conversation if you have honestly admitted that you are critical of others a good deal of the time.

It was Dr. James Dobson who suggested that we all need to develop the "no-knock policy." I hope he'll forgive me for borrowing his phrase, but it's been one of the most helpful suggestions I've ever heard. We were doing a seminar together when I first heard him talk about the no-knock policy. I jolted upright in my chair, because I was instantly reminded that I had "knocked" myself three times that very evening! They were small digs at my abilities and, while it did not hurt anyone else, it clearly revealed the feelings of inadequacy that were on my mind. It also told me I had said those negative things about myself in hopes that someone else would say, "Oh, no, Joyce, you are wrong about yourself . . . " and then they would praise me in the process. This "no-knock" policy is akin to "no insults" and includes no insults even to our own person-hood.

While a young mother was telling me about an incident she'd had over disciplining her children, she said, "There I was—dumb, stupid me, standing . . . " Then, not two minutes later she added, "Well, you know, I'm such a screwball and so disorganized, I . . . "

Our conversation was interrupted, and I was sorry I had no opportunity to introduce her to the no-knock policy.

Adopting the no-knock policy works like this: Every time you would say something negative or critical about yourself, your mate, your children, your neighbor, friends, business acquaintances, anyone . . . you refuse to say it. You crush it while it's still in the thought stage.

Remember, we are going to answer to God, and not for anyone else's actions, words, or deeds . . . just our own. So, our critical, harmful opinions do nothing but slam back rather hard on us. Try to forget your bad past and bury last year's failures. Accept forgiveness for your life, and recognize the moment when you should command your tongue to silence.

A guest author on a talk show was asked how she handled being a brand new stepmother. She drew a deep breath and then answered, "Most of the time, I smile and keep quiet. Then I smile again. And again. And again."

Yes, I'm well aware that confrontation is called for at specific times in our relationships with others, but there are many more *years* of just smiling, keeping quiet, and responding with the "no-knock" policy.

Peter says, "So get rid of your feelings of hatred. Don't pretend to be good! Be done with dishonesty and jealousy and talking about others behind their backs" (1 Peter 2:1).

Hard to do? You bet! Some of us have been habitually critical for years, so the habit might be difficult to break. But we can if we put our minds to it!

If you could play back a tape of all your conversations covering the past four weeks, what would the percentages of critical comments total? Would thirty percent be the sum and total of all derogatory remarks about yourself and others? Or would fifty percent of your sentences be negative statements about someone? I have asked myself these questions, and I was alarmed at my estimate of my own record.

Proverbs 11:17 says, "Your own soul is nourished when you are kind; it is destroyed when you are cruel."

I do not want to stand by and see the beauty of my soul or yours be destroyed by this disfiguring habit. We must exercise this no-knock policy in dealing with ourselves. We must practice this policy toward our husbands and, if we want to teach it to our children, we must practice the no-knock policy on them. They learn much more by catching than teaching.

> Drop, abandon, and abolish phrases like:
> "Billy is my two-year-old monster."
> "Sue certainly is a scrawny little thing."
> "You always make me mad."
> "You spoiled brat; stop that!"
> "You are so stupid."
> "Shut up!"

My mother was forty-five years old when she gave birth to my sister, Marilyn. But, to her everlasting credit, I never heard her introduce my sister as "This is Marilyn, our little surprise package. Ha! Ha!" or, "Meet Marilyn, our little caboose. Ha! Ha!" She would not degrade or knock her children publicly or privately.

We must specifically train our children not to knock themselves, their brothers or sisters, or us.

When Dr. Dobson and I were speaking together at weekend seminars called *Family Forum*, on one particular night he talked (again) about the no-knock policy. But this time the meeting was in Southern California and Laurie had driven me there. During a mid-evening break, I was talking to a woman when Laurie came up behind me. The area where I was standing was cramped and there was only a narrow aisle between the seats and the wall. When Laurie passed me, she lightly patted me on the hips and gaily whispered, "My, we're spreading out a little here, aren't we?"

It was no big deal, but I'd turned forty and, for the first time in my life, I weighed one hundred and fifteen pounds (and I wasn't pregnant). I laughed at the moment, but on the drive home I told Laurie that I knew I was being silly and immature but that her remark had stung a little. She didn't say too much but we did talk about adopting the no-knock policy.

The next night after I'd been speaking and during the break, Laurie handed me this note.

"Mom, I'm really sorry I teased you about being big in the hips. I do want you to know, you look beautiful tonight, and you are a truly beautiful woman. I want to strive to be the mother you are to Rick and to me. (I think that's terrible wording, I'm sure you understand what I mean.) You are what I will be some day . . . a fascinating woman. I love you, Mom."

It was an appropriate lesson for both of us. (Besides, I made up my mind to do daily exercises and take off inches in the hip area. It took two months, but, you know, when a woman makes up her mind . . .) Now that I'm in my fifties, I've put it all back on and a few pounds more. It's like Erma Bombeck's line, "Over the years I've lost two thousand pounds."

The third trait of a poised woman indirectly involves her mind but more directly concerns her body and physical posture.

3.   *She has learned to walk tall.*

When a woman is in the right relationship with God, she allows the Holy Spirit to control and work in her life, and she walks spiritually like a giant. When you talk with her, God seems to speak through her to you. You are impressed by His presence when you see her.

Dr. Billy Graham called Henrietta Mears "one of the greatest Christians I have ever known." I felt exactly the same way. I knew her only the last four years of her life, but she was a giant. I am five feet, six inches tall and I looked down at Miss Mears; but the second she spoke, I had to look up—way up. Always she turned my eyes off of her face and up to Jesus. It was an uncanny thing. She was a real person, humorous and intelligent, and yet I always felt I should take my shoes off when I was around her, as if I were standing on holy ground.

When Miss Mears was in a room, I just *knew* the Lord was sure to be right there. Close. Spiritually, she walked tall, and physically (though she was not much over five feet) she walked tall and elegantly, like a beautiful, gracious queen. Everything stopped when she entered a room, and each person in the room shared the single thought, *She's here! And she sees me!*

By contrast, Miss Mears did not enter the room with an attitude that said, "Here I am, you lucky people. I'm what you have been waiting for!" but with astounding humility that said, "Oh, here you are! I've been looking for you. How wonderful to see you!" There was a triumphal spring to her walk. Her posture and grooming were marvelous.

I spent my entire childhood hearing my father say, "Joyce, straighten up!" Often my mother lightly touched my shoulder blades and said one word, "Up."

Once a teacher tried to improve my posture by telling me to think of someone holding one or two strands of my hair straight up, and to pretend that I was being suspended from the ceiling as I walked. Another suggested I carry my bosom higher. None of those suggestions seemed to work.

Then, on several occasions, I saw Miss Mears walk into a room, and each time this tiny, yet dynamic woman fascinated me. I began to study her. I discovered that she did not enter like I did, nor like anyone else, for that matter.

I usually burst or exploded into a room. I brought the hurry, fatigue, and general disappointments of the day

with me. I always led my body with my head and shoulders. (I still do when I forget these lessons.)

The best advice I've ever read on posture and walking
is in a chapter called, "She Walks in Beauty" from a book
by Marjorie Frost.

> Maintain your good posture every step of the way
> to your chair after you've entered a room. This is one
> of the most important times to remember to lead with
> your thighs, because of a tendency to lean the body
> way forward and to bend the knees as if sitting, thus
> giving a "sitting walk" demonstration all the way to
> the chair.[2]

Most of us know we are to hold our head high and
relax the shoulders down, but to lead with the *thighs* is
a new concept. It's a great principle to walk by because
it puts our whole body in a nice perpendicular line of
graciousness and poise.

Miss Mears had this concept down to a fine science.
She brought warmth, enthusiasm, and unrestricted joy into
any room by the way she simply walked into it.

Her clothes and grooming were slightly spectacular.
She dressed as if she were God's daughter, as if she really
believed that God, the King, was her Father. Even in her
childhood, her mother had certain dresses and shoes that
Henrietta was allowed to wear only on Sunday to God's
house. I am not saying she spent enormous amounts of
money on clothing, but I am saying that whatever she wore
was in perfect taste and absolutely becoming to *her*.

Once, when she was talking about grooming, Miss
Mears suggested that we, in the privacy of our bedrooms,

---

[2] *Charming You*, Zondervan Publishing House, Grand Rapids,
Michigan.

dressing rooms, or wherever it was private, check each detail of personal grooming. She said that we should be as perfect as we could by "checking it all out" at the mirror *before* we left home. Then, we'd be able to walk out into the world and completely forget the whole thing. We didn't need to be self-conscious about our looks if we gave careful attention to our grooming before we stepped outside.

You might even want to check your looks right now in a verbal mirror. Are you one of the following three women?

A.   You go to the grocery store to do your shopping, dressed in your "absolute grubbies," and topping off the whole mess, your hair is rolled up in super-size pink rollers. You may not know it, but for all to clearly see is a sign above your head. It follows wherever you go and it says, "I do not like myself. I am rebelling over this stupid, boring job of buying groceries. I am showing my resentment of being a woman, a wife or a mother and of life in general by looking my ugliest!"

One high school instructor said, "I always understand why a girl is like she is after I've seen her mother at the market in rollers and hair curlers."

B.   Or maybe this sounds familiar. You show up at church in a dress that was designed for a seventeen-year-old girl who is a size seven. It's been ten years since you've been seventeen, and you've never been down to a size ten, much less a seven. Besides that, all the extra pounds you kept after the last baby was born stayed on your hips and upper thighs. Your short skirt waves around your chubby thighs like a ridiculous flag. You are a grooming disaster because you are trying to dress like someone else (a younger, junior-figured girl), and everybody but you knows it.

C.   Or, maybe you're just at home cooking dinner,

but you look so untidy and unappealing that you would spoil anyone's appetite. You wonder why your family is not happy during dinner, why they gulp their food down without conversation, and why the dinner hour is better known at your house as the "disaster hour."

None of these three types of women I've described have learned to walk tall. Any inner self-acceptance they may have once had has dried up and blown away. Their outward grooming, their posture, and their walk all speak of their lack of inner joy.

The woman who inwardly accepts God's forgiveness, likes herself on God's terms, and reflects the no-knock policy . . . walks in beauty. She creates this visual picture:

> She has clean and shining hair,
> Her makeup is not heavy but soft and feminine,
> She cares for her fingernails regularly and beautifully,
> Her teeth are clean and healthy,
> She has regular medical checkups each year,
> She uses a daily deodorant and radiates personal cleanliness,
> Her fragrance is definite but gentle and sweet,
> She exercises regularly and sticks to a diet,
> Her whole wardrobe fits her budget . . . and her body,
> She uses color to its best advantage,
> She avoids unladylike positions and moves with grace.

This outward appearance combines with her inner traits, and we see that she walks:

> According to God's commands.   Psalm 1 TLB
> Obediently.   Jeremiah 7:23 KJV
> Relaxed, because she travels "a good path."
>   Jeremiah 6:16 TLB

In safety.   Proverbs 2:7,9 TLB
In newness of life.   Romans 6:4 TLB
Without guilt.   Romans 8:1 TLB
With mercy and peace.   Galatians 6:16 TLB
With honesty.   Romans 12:3 TLB
In love, following Christ.   Ephesians 5:2 TLB
In freedom.   1 Peter 2:16 TLB

The tall woman looks ethereally lovely because of God's harmonious, well-balanced loveliness shining all about her.

She walks in flawless perfection, shimmering with the lights of His beauty.

Additional Scripture references for this chapter.

God loved you   Psalm 18:18,19 TLB
                                    Psalm 59:10 TLB
                                    Jeremiah 31:3 TLB

God made you   Acts 17:24-28 TLB
                                    1 Peter 4:19 TLB

God's plan for you   Psalm 103:1,5,8-10,12,13 TLB
                                    Psalm 147:5 TLB
                                    Ephesians 1:5,7,9-13 TLB
                                    Ephesians 2:10 TLB
                                    Hebrews 4:13,15 TLB

God's walk for you   Psalm 119:5,9 TLB
                                    Proverbs 13:20 KJV
                                    1 John 1:7 TLB

EIGHT

Anger: Mad As a
Wet Hen

I have always been aware of the fire burning deep inside me. It has smoldered and flared with varying degrees of temperature over the years.

When I was little and in grade school, I kept those fires my own, private secret. Whenever the angry, resentful flames flared up, I silently drowned them out with my tears. In fact, I cried so much that my father's often repeated and favorite line was, "Joyce flushes easily." Each time a person or problematic circumstance frustrated me, I handled it by crying. I managed to cry my way through junior high, high school, and college. Some days I'm still doing it.

Something happened to those fires after a few years of marriage and two children. They began to burn fiercely, and, more often than I cared to admit, raged out of control. The long-quiet, smoldering coals burst forth and erupted like a forceful volcano. Besides crying, I began spewing my anger verbally over everyone and everything.

I don't know where the phrase "mad as a wet hen" came from or exactly how it got started but I do know,

This hen,
When wet,
Gets mad!

At first I blamed it on my nationality, or rather my parents' nationalities. My mother was Hungarian and my father, Irish. Both nationalities were suitable candidates for the "hot-temper" reputation. I remember excusing my outbursts by saying with a touch of nationalistic pride, "Well, you know the Hungarians and the Irish—how could I be any other way?" (Others have blamed their red hair or their Uncle Fred.)

Sometimes I excused my hostile behavior by explaining, "It is better to get it all out into the open. Explode and get it over with." I was proud that I didn't hold grudges. It never occurred to me that I had left shattered people in the wake of my tongue lashings.

After a few years of trying unsuccessfully to excuse my temperamental outbursts, I simply reverted to blaming everyone else. Some time ago, I saw a woman who vividly reminded me of those days. I was standing in line behind her in the post office, waiting to mail a package. It was crowded and rushed because of the holiday season, and the wait was long. Just as the woman stepped up to the clerk's window, a man came in the front door, went to the side of the window, and said (over the woman's shoulder), "Hi, Bill, do you have my meter ready?"

The postman looked up and answered, "Sure, Bob!" and handed the meter to him.

The whole business took just under four seconds, but it was all that poor lady needed to explode into a furious rage. She slammed her fist down on the counter and yelled, "Who does he think he is? I was here first; I was next in line! Where does he get off—barging in front of me? I was first!"

The startled, somewhat shaken clerk put up both hands and tried to calm her by saying, "Lady, lady, it's all right. It just took a second ... Now, how can I help you?"

She leaned through the window, over the counter, and shook her finger in his face. "Who are you, to take his side?" she yelled. "I was here first! I've got things to do and places to go. Just shut your mouth and give me some stamps!"

All of us in that crowded postal substation were highly amused by the ridiculous scene the woman was creating. It was funny, because here she was—a grown woman—jumping up and down, pounding her fist, and screaming her lungs out over such a trivial, meaningless thing.

I was smiling right along with everyone else until I very distinctly heard a still small voice within me say, "What are you laughing at? I have seen *you* act exactly the same way." The Lord's words caught my breath, and I stopped smiling.

I took a closer look at the woman who was still ranting and raving, and I felt as if I were viewing a television instant replay of my own soul from some years back.

I saw myself as that horrible, disgusting lady. It had been a long time since I'd exploded like that, but perhaps God let me see this angry woman to remind me of what I could still be. Maybe I needed to remember to keep my heart sensitive and understanding to those who suffer from hostile, flaming eruptions in their souls.

I feel almost certain that woman left the post office that day, went home, and told her husband how awful she had been treated. She probably blamed everybody there for her conduct and her words.

We all suffer in this culture from a scary syndrome called "When-anything-goes-wrong." A lost-job; a failed-marriage; a sick-loved-one or a death-in-the-family ... Who's to blame?" We'll run uphill and backwards to fix the blame elsewhere.

I remember blaming everyone else, too. I'd say,

"My husband was insensitive to my needs."
"My children were impossible."
"The mailman was curt and rude."
"The neighbor doesn't like me."
"That salesman cheated me."
"The bank teller started the argument."

It was never my fault. I only started screaming after someone else had provoked me. I staunchly maintained my innocence and was very defensive about the whole matter. I lived out each day in anger. I was mad at God, mad at myself, mad at others, and fit to be tied with the angry frustrations of life in general.

Anger, during those disastrous years wrote its name across my face in hard, dark, indelible lines. It announced to the world that it was my master controller. For me, looking into a mirror was an awful thing each day because I could see the creeping ugly lines of anger aging my face. I not only feared growing old, but I was furious because I could see it happening. I was in my early twenties but my face was aging at an alarming rate!

What anger did to my looks, however, was nothing compared to the atrocities it perpetrated on my emotions and my mind. Every outburst of temper took its unbelievable toll on my character and personality.

As a woman, I became closed-minded and opinionated about everyone from the butcher to the women in the P.T.A. I made instant judgments and assumptions on everything from convenience foods to politics. (I must have been a colossal bore!)

To our children, I became a rather strict, overbearing, tyrannical mother who threatened them daily with, "Don't you make me mad or I'll lose my temper and you'll be sorry!" (From my children's ground level, I must have loomed before them like an ugly fire-breathing giant-mother-monster.)

It is not pleasant for me to remember and write about my anger. Yet, I know some of you will read and identify with the honest descriptions of anger and will begin, maybe for the first time, to see unvarnished ugliness.

I wish I could say that the Lord just simply stepped in and *removed* my anger, my resentment, and my flaming temper. But that's simply not true to the way God works; nor is it true to the real way life here on this planet works.

Anger is real. It is an emotion you have before you accept Christ and one you still have after you accept Him. It's as natural as my being five feet, six inches tall when I came to Christ and still measuring five feet, six inches after I've asked Him into my heart. (I may have grown taller spiritually in these years, and I pray so, but at first, it was plain ole five feet, six inches before *and* after.) Somehow, we have it in our heads that *good Christians* are not supposed to feel angry. Nor is any *good Christian* suppose to express anger at me.

I do not believe it is wrong to experience anger. We should recognize and accept anger as a normal, valid emotion. We can have anger, but if anger has us, then that's a different story. If anger controls us, it twists and warps every facet of our personalities and *that is wrong. It is sin.*

I said earlier in this chapter that I had an inner fire within me. I still do, even though I've been a Christian for many years. I am capable of showing that fire at any time.

I was discussing with a Christian woman what place anger has or does not have in the lives of Christian women, and at one point she said, "I wouldn't give you two cents for a woman if she didn't have that inner fire in her."

When the Lord got me, he got the inner fire, too. However, in order to make Christ my Lord, Savior, and King, I had to move the inner fires of anger off of the throne of my life. I had to dethrone and devaluate my anger. It no longer could have first place in the center of my being, and it could no longer run my life or make decisions for me. It was not easy in those early days of being a Christian to objectively (and correctly) assess the damage anger had already wrought on my soul, but I began to try. I couldn't see myself, as a Christian woman, constantly losing my temper. I realized that there would be times when someone (or something) could rouse the anger in me, but blowing my top in a temper tantrum seemed to be inappropriate and in very poor taste for a woman newly born in Christ.

In looking back over the frustrations and resentments that seemed to trigger my angry outbursts, I found two very distinct kinds of anger. It is important to look carefully and prayerfully at both of them. How successfully you handle the emotion of anger may be determined by what you discover about anger's nature. One type of anger is destructive and ugly, whereas the other type can actually bring healing or creative changes. Here is the ugly, dreadful type of anger.

1. *Personal anger*

This ego-shattering kind of anger always involves what someone did or said to *me*. It's always a case of feeling *personally* abused. For instance, I was resentful and angry because someone else . . .

> got the job I wanted.
> recorded albums.
> wrote books.
> sang solos in church.
> got pay raises.
> won recognition.
> were appreciated.
> looked beautiful.

I was angry and hurt because my loved ones . . .

> misunderstood my motives.
> failed to be perfect (there's a good one!).
> cramped my style.

noticed my lack of cooking and cleaning skills.

griped about my lack of cooking and cleaning skills.

didn't appreciate me and told me so.

As you can see, most of my anger was the personal kind. In all fairness to myself, I must say that once in a while I did suffer a real injustice and that I had a few honest moments of anger, but it was a rare occurrence.

My reactions to these assaults to my ego were always wild arpeggios of anger. I allowed the destructive qualities of anger to dictate my actions. My wounded pride was usually at the core of my anger.

This next type of anger is a world removed from personal anger.

2.   *Virtuous anger*

This anger is a loving, caring, sinless kind of emotion that involves our being angry because of an injustice or wrong done to *someone else*. If we will use this virtuous anger in a loving way, we can become true agents of reconciliation in a world that's torn and splitting apart.

That's the hang-up though. Most of us are not angry about injustices involving others. Our anger is so self-centered that we rarely get mad for someone else. As an apathetic generation, we have forgotten what bridges can be built by loving, caring, sinless anger.

One of the most enriching adventures in music I've ever had started by exercising this kind of anger.

During a Sunday morning church service, I was looking up at the nearly two-hundred college students scattered around the balcony, and I got mad. I was angry because we had a huge church with thousands of members and we had children's choirs and adult choirs but no collegiate singing group. There were all those kids sitting in the balcony on all that unused potential. I was angry enough to go see our minister of music, Rollie Calkin.

After I'd poured out my heart-concern and urgently pleaded for a college folk-rock group to be started, I finished with, "*Somebody* has got to do something with these college kids!"

Rollie said, "Right! *You* do it!." (I had in mind Rollie's doing something—not me!).

It's been many years now since I organized and directed those beautiful kids, but the group known as the "Overtones" continued on. They've given hundreds of concerts, recorded an album or two, and have influenced hundreds of young people to trust in Christ. It all began with virtuous anger, a wise minister of music, and pure determination.

We tend to think of Jesus as always turning the other cheek, as being meek and mild, but that's not a totally complete picture. Jesus did get angry. He was very definitely "mad as a wet hen" when He threw the money changers out of the temple. But His anger always seemed to be this second kind—this virtuous kind.

Mark 3:4,5 reveals Jesus had enemies; He was talking to some of them in that passage. After they wouldn't answer His questions, Mark describes Jesus as "looking around at them *angrily*, for He was deeply disturbed by their indifference to human need . . . " So Jesus was angry, but Mark clearly labels the type of anger. Jesus was not angry at the people but at their attitude of indifference!

Dr. Henry Brandt helped me understand about the spirit of love and the spirit of anger. He clearly set down the principle that if I was filled with the spirit of love, nothing could make me angry. If I, in turn, was filled with the spirit of anger, practically anything could make me angry.

In the years that have followed, the truth of those words has become a reality. When I daily ask the Lord to fill me with His spirit of love, the ugly personal anger (involving ego) simply does not get a chance to work its poison. On the other hand, the sinless kind of anger (involving others) can lovingly be used in creative ways— healing and restoring as it goes along.

Only twice in those years did it not work that way. Both times the episodes involved my father and what he was doing (or not doing) to my sister, Marilyn. Both times my talking to him *began* quietly with sinless anger and righteous, virtuous concern on my part for my sister. Both times I failed to be the Christian I should have been. Somewhere, in both conversations, I lost (or dropped) my sinless anger concept and succumbed to personal anger. It proves that, while one may start in the spirit of love, it's possible to slip unconsciously under the control of an angry spirit.

"Don't you *ever* get mad at your children?" one mother of four asked. Of course, I get mad, but I try to get mad at what they have done—the deed—and not at them individually. If I get hung up on what they have *done to me*, my temper will always be simmering just below the boiling point. None of what I'm saying comes as second nature to anyone, so it's a constant thing of adjusting my attitude and releasing my anger to the Lord.

When Laurie put a long single scratch down the entire length of my car, she knew I was mad. Boy was I mad! However, losing my temper, screaming and yelling, "You stupid girl, how could you have managed to scratch the entire length of the car?" would never have erased the damage, nor would it have helped Laurie to move past the damage my words would have done to her soul.

Nothing is ever accomplished by wild anger. It is pretty futile to let anger control us. It might have felt good, for a second or two, to yell at Laurie and release some tension, but what real good would that have done? Is the portrait of a screaming, hysterical mother the one I want her to carry into adulthood? Do I want her to picture her growing-up time at home as a period of failures, accidents, and mistakes with a yelling mother superimposed over it all?

Laurie knew I was angry, hurt, and just plain "sick" over that scratch, simply by the look on my face. All I said was a quiet, "Oh, Laurie." Nothing more was needed. Firing my temper like an immature sore loser would have never given me the elaborate, sincere, heartfelt apology from Laurie the next day. The biggest victory comes though, when you realize that if you are angry at the problem and not the person, you are free from that hard knot of anger usually located in the pit of your stomach on days like that.

God knows there will be days when we will experience anger. There will even be days when we will fail to be in control of that anger (like the two experiences with my father). But God also knows that if He can help us to channel our anger, we will be healthier, freer, and wiser.

God is careful to warn us about potential danger in anger. The Bible states, "Be ye angry and sin not" (Ephesians 4:26). Watch out for that personal kind of anger—that's usually the kind we sin over. Then, direct your anger to the problem—not to the person.

If you are a woman whose life constantly displays the illness of chronic hostilities, I know you are suffering, but it isn't fatal. And it isn't too late for the cure. You have a temperament. We all do. But, you *can* live without a destructive temper. Read these wise, healing words of Paul:

If you are angry, be sure it is not out of wounded pride or bad temper [*personal anger*]. Never go to bed angry, don't give the devil that sort of foothold. Let there be no more resentment, no more anger, or temper, no more violent self-assertiveness, no more slander and no more malicious remarks [*more personal anger*]. Be kind to each other; be understanding. Be as ready to forgive others as God for Christ's sake has forgiven you (Ephesians 4:26,27,31,32 PH).

The portrait of us which our children should carry into adulthood is described in the last sentences. Will their picture of us be one of kindness, understanding, and forgiveness?

The whole world is looking longingly for this kind of beautiful woman. They are sick to death with the hatred and anger written across the faces of most people today.

God's woman has a fantastic source of beauty right at her elbow. She has a master cosmetologist beside her to erase the hard lines of anger. With a touch of His hand, He can soften her rigid skin into the beautiful flawless complexion of kindness. He rejuvenates her cheek bones by gently brushing them with the fresh glow of understanding. Her mouth glistens with the ointment of gentleness. He lets the inner fire of her soul add extra sparkle to her eyes, and they are bright with forgiveness. When He is finished with His work, He sends her out into the world He made, turns the floodlights up, and we all see *she is a beauty.*

Yours eyes light up your inward being. A pure eye lets sunshine into your soul. A lustful eye shuts out the light and plunges you into darkness. So watch out that the sunshine isn't blotted out. If you are filled with light within, with no dark corners, then your face will be radiant too, as though a floodlight is beamed upon you (Luke 11:34-36).

Additional Scripture references for this chapter.

Our behavior   Proverbs 10:14,19 TLB
                        Proverbs 12:16 TLB
                        Proverbs 18:1,2 TLB
                        Proverbs 28:13 TLB
                        Proverbs 29:22 TLB
                        1 Corinthians 16:4 TLB
                        2 Corinthians 6:3,4 TLB
                        Ephesians 6:15-17 TLB
                        1 John 3:18 TLB

NINE

The Gracious Beauty of Forgiveness and Love

I know of another woman, such as I've described in the previous chapter, who lived out each day of her life in anger. She had accepted Christ many years ago, but had never grown in the Lord or kept her personal relationship to Him clear and open. She allowed little sins (nothing ever bigger than a white lie or a mini-gossip session) to pile up year after year. By the time she was in her mid-forties, she was a disaster to be around. We all wondered how her husband put up with it.

She displayed all the symptoms of the angry, out-of-the-right-relationship-with-God person. She had few (if any) real friends, no outside-the-home interests (no inside-the-home interests, either); so all of her attention was focused inwardly on herself. She was full of the poor-me attitude in public, and nagged her husband to death in private. (I should say, "semi-private" because we got in on a few remarks one night at dinner with them.)

Then suddenly, almost over night, she changed. My! How she changed! She was a different person and was a delight to be around, but we could hardly believe our eyes. Then someone told me that after years of his wife's nagging, haranguing, arguing, and tongue lashing, the woman's husband turned to her one day and said, "What exactly is it that I have done to cause you to be this way? I must be responsible for at least part of your angry outbursts, so please tell me. I'd like to stop doing that to you." (No, this is not a trumped-up fairy tale ... it really happened.)

His wife listened in stunned silence, and then wept as he said, "Will you forgive me for what I've done to you? Will you forgive me for failing to be the husband I should have been to you?"

When the wife was faced with such forgiving, loving kindness, she melted. Who wouldn't? She also got a clear look at the basic problem, which was not her husband and his faults, but herself.

If you have just guessed that the opposite of anger is forgiveness, you have guessed correctly. If you go one step further, you will realize that when anger and hate are dissolved by forgiveness, real loving is free to begin!

The woman who heard her husband's genuine request for forgiveness had to go back to her own forgiveness from God and begin again. God then began (overnight) to change her. *First though, she had to forgive herself.*

If there was a formula for making my life work, it began with the incredible realization that I was allowing the sin of anger to spew forth daily in my life. I accepted the fact that I was responsible for most of the anger in my life and for a good many ugly responses that came from loved ones.

There is nothing like one human being saying to another, "Will you forgive me?" Nothing melts angry resentments like an apology.

There is a warm current of strength and substance running through an offered apology. "Will you forgive me?" has an honest humility about it that pours over our souls and soothes like some fragrant balm.

Once, when I was speaking in an Army chapel to some troops in Thailand, I was talking about asking this forgiving kind of question and I said, "Maybe someone right here needs to write a letter home to a mother, wife, or friend to ask, 'Will you forgive me?' "

I was somewhat startled by a soldier on the front row directly in front of me, who shot his hand in the air and said, "Excuse me, Ma'am, but I've got to say something. You're talking about me. It's me who's got to write that letter. Wait till I tell you!" He then told the whole group how his wife and he were ready to get a divorce. Every letter he'd received from her had sent him to his pad of paper to fire off one angry page after another back to her. The last letter he had received from his wife arrived that morning, and he had been waiting all day to write her one dandy, final sign-off letter.

His buddy, seated next to him, had convinced him to come to my evening meeting at the chapel. He had sat there all through the musical part of my performance, just stewing over the letter he was going to write. But when I began to talk, the Lord started revealing to him the real cause of his problem. As he began to form some definite conclusions, he simply *had* to interrupt me. He was just beautiful as he said, "I've got to write my wife; I've got to ask her forgiveness. So many of our problems are my fault, not hers. I never saw that before. I've got to get right with God, too. It's been a long time since I've asked His forgiveness!"

He said some other things, but I couldn't see him because of my tears, and I couldn't hear him because of the joyous bells that were ringing somewhere deep inside me.

Some of us have never tried asking for forgiveness. Oh, we've said, "I'm sorry," but we've said it without truthful conviction to enforce it. We are too proud, too stubborn, or too sure it won't work, and we refuse to see our responsibility in the situation.

Others of us have never seen that we have any fault or blame for the problem. We need desperately to confess our faults one to another and then, with God's help ask, "Will you forgive me?"

I am painfully aware that asking forgiveness and forgiving others is not easy. The guidelines and principles for forgiveness are not simplistic or easily learned. It's far easier to practice them once and then forget them. Forgiveness must be kept up to date, but, when it is, life takes on new and different dimensions every day.

It will take every ounce of energy and brains you've got to keep your marriage and your children growing. You will never run out of occasions to use these guidelines; new opportunities arise all the time. I do know, however, from experience, that these principles can be applied and they *do work.*

A woman can muddle through her problems feeling angry and confused. She can suffer as a victim of "terrible circumstances." She can "live through" her problems. But I recommend "loving through" instead. We can love our way through confusion into peace. We can learn to understand the real issues in life. We can even understand ourselves in these issues.

Here are some guidelines, and I pray they will be helpful and practical.

1.   *Realize you cannot change some things.*

The woman who has let anger rob her of her beauty is most easily identified by the way she *pounces.*

She pounces on relatives, mate, children, past events and future events faster than you can blink an eye. She critically pounces on any unobtainable or unrealistic goals in her life or yours. Heaven help you if your nose is too big or too small, because she loves to pounce on a person's physical characteristics.

The woman of forgiveness sees the same problems, the same people, and even the same noses. Yet, she makes up her mind *to accept them all*. There are just a great number of things, people, and circumstances that cannot be changed. The woman of beauty accepts things which cannot be altered, and she accepts them *without* a martyr complex. She can be sensitive and alert to the needs of others because she has known God's forgiveness and love in those same areas of her life.

Most of us are willing to accept a person's good traits. Few of us are willing to look at and love a person with the less than loveable traits. But the truth is you may not be able to change

> your husband's stubbornness . . . or his snoring.
> your son's acne . . . or his messy room.
> your daughter's height . . . or her love of old jeans
> your mother-in-law's set ways . . . or her remarks.
> your parents' attitudes . . . or lack of attitudes.
> your financial problem . . . except by burning your credit cards.
> your physical disabilities . . . or your new bifocals

So why bother? Remember this famous prayer?

> God, grant me the serenity
> To accept the things I cannot change,
> Courage to change the things I can,
> And the wisdom to know the difference.

It's highly possible that God will not change certain people in your life. Nor will they change on their own. God may not take away problems, but, if He doesn't, don't be discouraged. He will give you just enough relaxed grace to accept them, to live with them, and perhaps even to love them. (Read 2 Corinthians 12:9. It's a promise!)

Henrietta Mears, who had terrible vision problems, often said, "I believe my greatest spiritual asset throughout my entire life has been my failing sight, for it has kept me absolutely dependent on God!" Now there was a beautiful woman! She accepted her loss, and was grateful for it, because it kept her in the right relationship with God.

2. *Realize you will have differences.*

I worry just a little when a couple confidently states, "We *never* have an argument." All this really says is that (1) they are lying, or (2) one of them has given up all his or her rights, ideas, opinions, and thoughts and goes through life door-mat style.

We all tend to presume that so-and-so doesn't have arguments or conflicts in his life. We are especially sure of that if so-and-so is named Billy Graham or if so-and-so is a minister or missionary. (Even some authors are accused of "having it made.") We must stop putting people (even "spiritual giants") on pedestals, because they are human and they *do have conflicts*. We all do.

Because God has made each of us uniquely different, we will always have some areas of disagreement. We may even have outright conflicts, but we no longer need to scream our vengeance at one another or run away from our problems.

Once when I was hurt by a remark someone repeated four times in my presence, I let everyone there know the truth. I charged in to "right" every wrong by explaining everything. The "forgiven" me asked God for better timing, a clean heart, and a right spirit. Later, when the time was right, I would tell the person I was hurt and that I knew it was silly of me, but I needed to talk with him about our differences. (It would have been easier to have swept the whole thing under the rug and not mention it. But I know from experience that if I did that, I'd sneak back every day, lift up the rug, and poke around in the dirt.)

After we talked over the minor problem and worked out a solution, our relationship was strengthened, but it started with admitting that there was a difference of opinion and then doing something about it.

The wise woman of beauty waits for God's timing, and then privately discusses the issues. She does not ridicule or even poke the digging type of humor at her husband in front of children, friends, or associates. She applies the same principle of privacy when she deals with her children's conflicts, whenever it's possible. And, most important, she attacks the problems, not the people. The wise woman of beauty accepts the challenge of reconciliation, and she becomes an expert in this next step.

3. *Resolve differences creatively.*

David Augsburger said, "Resolving conflict creatively is the result of love-in-action. Love is something you do. It must be expressed in all three levels of communication: the verbal (I love you), the nonverbal (I feel with you, I truly hear you), and the symbolic (I give to you)."[1]

The woman who does not want to bother with settling anything creatively ... who is too self-centered to want to take the time, the effort, or pay the price that creative living costs finds it's easier to just blow up, to say what's on her mind. She stands by and lets the chips fall where they may. She feels a bit guilty afterwards but justifies her words and angry actions by saying, "Well, I can forgive so-and-so but I'll never forget. After all, look what *he* did to me!"

The woman who would solve the daily problems and differences in her life by using a creative method is very beautiful.

I asked one beautiful woman if she had a temper. "Very definitely, but most of the time it's under control,"

---

[1] *Cherishable: Love and Marriage*, Herald Press, Scottdale, PA.

she answered. I asked her how that had been accomplished in her life. As accurately as I can recall, this was her answer:

"All my life has been filled with large problems. The Lord has allowed me to experience every kind of hurt and trial imaginable. Never once, at any time or in any way, has another human being been able to solve those problems. No one has come up with any solutions. So, for a long time now I've gone only to the Lord with my troubles. He is the only one capable of solving things. I take my anger over a person or a problem immediately to the Lord. I tell Him I've no one but Him, and He in turn gives me the control I need for that moment."

Then, thoughtfully, she added later, "You know, I suspect that a good many Christian women are too sheltered from real problems, so they've developed no spiritual muscles. They are too weak and powerless to cope with problems. They really don't believe God can help, but oh, He can and does."

If only Christian women would think of their problems as spiritual muscle builders, we might have churches full of strong, vibrant, healthy women. Homes might be filled with the savory aroma of forgiveness and love, and maybe we'd see faces glowing from the exquisite beauty of God's love.

"Yes, Joyce," you say, "but what you are saying is not so easily done. It's hard to be forgiving and loving."

That's right, it *is* hard. But who said it would be easy? Who said that if you become a Christian you automatically become an expert in loving? Not I!

Peter gave us a clue as to how it's done when he said, "Now you can have real love for everyone because your souls have been cleansed from selfishness and hatred when you trusted Christ to save you; so see to it that you really do love each other warmly, with all your hearts" (1 Peter 1:22).

He gave two points for loving. Remember you've been forgiven, and then see to it that you love! (Back to "Make up your mind, Lady!)

But none of this is done easily or naturally. In fact, the forgiving kind of loving costs us a great deal. It may cost us everything we have.

We all know it's very expensive and time consuming
    to apologize.
    to begin all over again.
    to be unselfish.
    to take advice.
    to admit error.
    to face criticism.
    to be charitable to the ungrateful.
    to keep on trying.
    to be considerate.
    to appreciate him or her.
    to avoid mistakes.
    to make allowances for others.
    to bear a personal insult.
    to believe the best about someone.
    to endure success.
    to profit by mistakes.
    to forgive by Christ's love and forget.
    to think and then to act.
    to keep out of the rut.
    to grow older.
    to make the best of little things.
    to maintain high standards.
    to give someone else grace.
    to understand someone's thoughtless blunder.
    to shoulder deserved blame.
    to subdue impulsive anger.
    to recognize a person's worth.
    to see the silver lining.
    to let the beauty of Christ be seen.

You see, these are very difficult and expensive things. It is not easy or cheap to love—*but it always pays!*

The world would have us believe that the greatest power known to man is force. The Lord has proved that the greatest force in the world is love. Love, His love, never fails. Have you seen it working in your face, your life, your home?

My daughter, Laurie, has always been cute and perky! She's charmed everyone for years with her darling, yet surprising personality. But now that she is a young wife and mother of two, she is a smashing beauty. Like most of us, she was not always so shimmering with loveliness. I recall somewhere in her fourteenth year when she had her own rebellion about everything from skirt lengths to hating peas and carrots. She made it very difficult for anyone to love her, and she casually, yet deliberately, drove me up the wall! For eighteen months, she doubted everything about the Lord, she disagreed with everything I said or did, and in general, she made life miserable. I refused to let any of her ugly actions affect my loving her—it wasn't easy, but somehow I managed, in spite of all she did.

Just when I was beginning to think I'd never see the end of this angry rebellion, she had her own very precious experience with the Lord. (God has no *grandchildren.*) I had insisted that she go on tour with our church high school choir. Very reluctantly, she went, and the first night changed her life forever. She was angry and mad at everyone from God on down to herself and everyone in between. But she was fed up mostly with herself, so she prayed, "Okay Lord, if You can be real, *be real to me!*"

God's bolt of lightning struck her, dead center, and she came home a changed girl. It took me six months to adjust to the new Laurie. I almost fainted when she came into the kitchen that first night home and said, "Oh, Mom, everything smells so wonderful! What's for dinner?"

I thank God that my mother never let my mean traits, ugly ways, or rebellious actions at sixteen convince her to stop loving or praying for me. It was a great lesson for me to remember when Laurie came along. I'm glad I followed my mother's example because what Laurie became is beautiful!

I've seen this forgiving, loving power of God transform Laurie. There is a joyous, radiant spirit shining like a halo around her head. It was best described by a boy named Mark, who came to pick up Laurie for a date at that time.

She was still getting ready, so Mark was chatting with me. He was in an involved explanation about something when the hall door opened and Laurie came through.

She was quite a picture. Her blonde hair was softly curled around her shoulders, her blue eyes were sparkling, and her slim size-seven figure was a delight to see. Mark stopped mid-sentence and no one moved while he took her all in; then he said very quietly, "Wow, Laurie, you look so soft . . ."

I've thought of that moment many times, because indeed she did look so soft, so gentle, and so lovely. I couldn't help but compare the old Laurie to the new Laurie. I remembered how anger had made her almost cruel looking at times. How hard her eyes had looked. But not now. The transformation was because of the gentle, softening action of God's forgiveness and love.

God's love never fails. Its softening ability is one of the biggest contributions to beauty a woman can experience. Have you seen it? It's a thing of beauty and a joy forever.

Additional Scripture references for this chapter. All of these references are found in The Living Bible.

Accept life	Psalm 13:5,6
	Psalm 15
	Psalm 37:1-9
	James 5:16
New life	Colossians 3:12-14
	James 1:19-21
	James 1:26
Try love, *you'll like it*	Romans 12:9,10
	James 4:11
	1 Peter 2:1-4
	1 Peter 4:8
	1 John 3:14-16
	1 John 3:18
	1 John 4:18,19
Future benefits *of loving*	Psalm 22:30
	Psalm 25:12,13
	Psalm 37:25,26

TEN

You and Your
Beautiful Personality

The rain alternates its sound level from a light drizzling patter to the heavy plopping drops of a down-pour, but other than that, my house is quiet. I'm writing this in my warm, comfortable living room, surrounded by books, papers, notes and clippings.

I can't help but wish that for this last chapter I could see you, talk with you, and wrap up this book with you— face to face.

There never seems to be enough time for that sort of thing, and I suppose it's unrealistic to think I could crowd you all into my living room, anyway. But I wish I could.

A few times in my life I've been able to have those special moments and do just that with a friend. Like times with Clare (the beautiful woman to whom this book is dedicated), when over a steaming cup of hot tea we have sat and shared, in the language of love, our thoughts about life in our world. Those times though, have been rare because of the schedules and the busyness of our lives.

Since the days of our ancestors, our busy pace has steadily increased. By now, we all whirl so much we need somebody (sometimes anybody) to stop the whirling. We

need to hold still for a minute and reflect on our beginnings. We need to share with someone some of the puzzling
mysteries of our lives and personalities.

Nowadays, there are no pot-bellied stoves in country
stores where we can voice our opinions loud and strong.
There are few, if any, quilting bees held in small church
circles where we can make small talk or trade confidences.
There are some small group meetings after church and
some small prayer groups, but not nearly enough to handle
the need for developing the personality God wants for us.

I don't really believe there is such a thing as a self-
made man (or woman). We need people. We need to grow
and develop, and to do that, we need to converse with each
other.

Strangely, though, there doesn't seem to be enough
time for the founding and nurturing of a slow, steady
friendship with someone who shares our ideals, backgrounds, and concerns. To have a friend with "history"
takes time and lots of shared experiences.

We seem to live out our lives as spectators at a drama
called *life*. Thanks to modern technology, we are besieged
with so much to entertain us, that even the art of conversation has lost much of its sparkle . . . and we are reduced
to small talk and mask wearing.

Sometimes women don't enjoy the company of other
women. That's basically because of two things relating to
conversation: (1) meaningless, prattling small talk and
(2) destructive, negative discussions. Even prayer meeting can be a disguised trap. We hear a lady request prayer
and she says, "We must pray for Debbie because . . . well
. . . you know she's having problems." (As a matter of
fact, I didn't know, and my mind doesn't hear the next
request because I'm still back on Debbie, wondering *"What
problems?"*

Because of busy schedules, women usually meet

in masses at various supermarkets, big parties, large churches, P.T.A., or women's meetings, and there's only time enough for a brief greeting.

"Did you have a good summer?"

"It seems like ages since I saw you last."

"I don't know where the time goes."

"I've been meaning to call you but ... "

The meaningless words rush and tumble out, and we only have time for thoughts off the top of our heads, hurried hands with quick hugs or no hug at all, and we hide our hearts. Subjects are lightly touched. Shown emotions are labeled as "sentimentality," and any prying beneath the surface is branded as bad manners.

So it is, that in our day we don't know very much about each other; and, conversely, nobody knows very much about us. What's worse, however, is that we know precious little about ourselves!

Once there was a time when we felt safe enough to spread ourselves, our thoughts, and our dreams around. We let off steam here, there, and everywhere, at least now and then. But now, that's not quite the thing to do. In fact, we are not too sure we have any steam any more. But we do! We have steam, we have emotions, and we even have hopes and dreams.

Human nature does not change. Yet, somewhere over the years the doors through which we used to walk freely into each other's hearts and minds have been shut and closed tightly.

There is much in us that is wonderful and awful, good and bad, which we do not understand or talk about. We presume no one ever had our specific problems, so we keep the scalding steam of inner conflicts all bottled up, and give it no place to blow off.

I remember, during my childhood, that my father's church had the practice of the "open altar." After the meeting, the altar area was open for anyone to come, kneel, pray, cry, or just be silent before the Lord. (My dearest memories are of my mother kneeling at the altar, praying, and quietly weeping before the Lord.) Somewhere along the path of growing up, I lost the open altar concept and closed an important channel of sharing with God or friend.

Now, out of our modern age and symbolic of it has come a new, highly specialized science. It's called psychiatry.

"Psychiatry," states William Glasser, "must be concerned with two basic psychological needs: (1) the need to love and be loved and (2) the need to feel that we are worthwhile to ourselves and to others."[1]

Careful, conscientious men and women are practicing this science. Christian psychologists and psychiatrists are among my dearest friends and co-workers, and I can rejoice over the results of their dedicated work.

Therapy from these gifted, listening people have helped some women back to wholeness and many a woman has been given direction in figuring out where and when conflicts began in her life. Often, when we are helped to mentally work and figure things out, we are freed from the frustrations of life that would keep us shut up as an emotional invalid.

Sometimes, though, in spite of a psychologist's, psychiatrist's, or counselor's dedicated efforts, we find people who just cannot accept healing. Other people won't go to a Christian doctor to begin with. Still others won't even admit there is a problem, so God's healing hand cannot cure them. Why?

My mother once gave me an illustration to help with this difficult "why." It went something like this. Your watch breaks, so you take it to a master watch repair specialist. He carefully takes your watch apart, spreads it

---

[1] *Reality Therapy*, Harper and Row, New York, NY.

on the work bench before him and gives you his quick "show-and-tell" lesson on why it doesn't work—the rusty spring here, the clogged and dirty wheel there, and a broken mainspring to name just a few of the problems. Slowly he cleans, mends, oils, replaces parts, and puts it all together again. He finishes it and hands your old watch back to you, not new, but repaired and working.

Now, I'm sure you'll understand the analogy. In the rush of life, your world breaks down and threatens to quit running altogether, so you take it to someone, a counselor or pastor, who has studied the conflicts of living. He or she helps you spread out your rusty emotions, your clogged-up sinful life, and your broken dreams on the table before you. But then, differing from the watch repairman, he says, "Now, here's what went wrong. What you have to do is pick up the pieces and put your life back into running order. I'll help you all I can, but *you must do it* yourself."

He gives you all sorts of encouragement but, somehow, you feel you just can't do it. You know you need something else . . . but what? You can't say . . . but it's just *something* else. I know this from my experiences.

Years ago I felt I had nobody to talk to, though I was surrounded with people who loved me and whom I loved. I would not go to a psychologist or counselor. I couldn't confide my inner conflicts to my husband, friends, or parents without it tearing them down and being very destructive. I was sure they wouldn't understand my conflicts, or that, worse, they would judge me for them. I was supposed to be a strong person, whether I wanted to be or not. A good psychologist could have pointed out the beginnings, the early, basic warning signs and the main spots of my conflicts, but I was not confident about that being the answer for me.

Even after I'd intellectually figured things out, seen

where I'd gone wrong, analyzed the problems in my past life and background, I *still* did not have any answers. To try and put the pieces of my life back together again was a cruel joke—an impossibility.

Many difficult emotions built up, and then increased, and finally multiplied. There was not room enough inside me, just as there is not room enough inside any of us, for all the terrors, the troubles, the longings, and the dreams. They have to spill over somewhere and on someone.

By the time I thought life was over, I had intellectually figured it all out, but had no cure and no real answers. I didn't know *I had to establish* a joint enterprise with God for the lasting cure.

All the answers to life's conflicts do not come from one friend, doctor, or counselor. It takes more.

If we are to begin to spread our thoughts, our dreams, our unacknowledged wickedness, our passing crazy fantasies, our hopes, our loves and hates out on a table, like pieces of a watch before a repair man, we must do it before someone who has within Him greater tolerance, greater comprehension, and supernatural powers of forgiveness. There is only one such person and that is GOD.

Years ago, alone, I went before God. He was the Master Designer who spread the pieces of my life out on the table, explaining the conflicts as He went along. Then, unlike the watch repairman or the counselor, it seemed to me that the Lord wiped the pieces off of the table with one sweeping motion, and said, tenderly, "Here, dear broken and battered child, take this. It's your new life—whole and complete. I did not come to patch and glue you back together again, but I've come to bring you a new life. I'll keep the wheels of your soul oiled with forgiveness; I'll wind the mainspring of your thoughts with My love; and you will live and tick away the seconds of this life with great hope, peace, and abundant joy!"

Most of our strength and will to live comes from being in a joint enterprise with God. There is always an answer to life's conflicts. Psychologists play an important part in helping us to see the troubled areas. I know and recommend a number of compassionate Christian counselors, but if your doctor does not ultimately point you to the all-forgiving God, then you will have only part of the answer and may never be cured. Unfortunately no doctor in the world can resolve the sin-caused conflicts within us. He can only point us in God's direction. It is God alone who can forgive.

A beautiful, openly honest personality begins with acknowledging our need and opening our minds, wills, and emotions to the God of answers. It may mean finding your own "open altar," kneeling before Him, and praying something like the following.

Dear God,

Here I am, problems and all. Forgive me. Forgive my sins. I'm worn out, broken, and I can't be patched up. I need a new life. Please come into my soul and touch me with Your healing hands. I want to exchange

my hates for Your loves.

my anger for Your forgiveness.

my insecurities for Your high evaluations.

my worry for Your words in prayer.

my fear for a measure of Your fadeless faith.

my bitterness for Your thanksgiving.

Now, thank You, Lord, for doing all this, even before I see the change or results. Amen.

The woman who prays this and accepts God's forgiveness can connect her spirit with God's. She can enter into a joint enterprise with the God who made her.

Her personality can begin to show some special traits and spiritual qualities. The inner beauteous glow can happen.

1.   *This woman has the fragrant sense of spiritual truths.*

She does not merely quote Bible truths, she transforms them into solid realities. Her daily reading of God's Word teaches her the fine art of Christian living. When she listens to you, she sees you as Christ would see you. When you look closely, you see that she glows with the gift of peace. Jesus said, "I am leaving you with a gift—peace of mind and heart! And the peace I give isn't fragile like the world gives. So don't be troubled or afraid" (John 14:27).

2.   *This woman has a sense of indescribable sweetness about her.*

This is not a saccharine, phony sweetness, but a genuine one. When you talk with her, you feel the presence of the altogether lovely One, and you know He is dear to her. She is like the beautiful, Dale Evans Rogers—actress, singer, and author—who was asked rather rudely if she'd had a surgical face lift. Dale just answered sweetly, "No, no face lift—just my heart."

3.   *This woman has the fragrant sense of victory over temptation.*

She very definitely admits to having temptations— big and small, but she has made up her mind to be habitually triumphant over them. She has taken the wise counsel of Paul to her heart and mind. He said, "I advise you to obey the Holy Spirit's instructions. He will tell you where to go and what to do, and then you won't always be doing the wrong things your evil nature wants you to do" (Galatians 5:16).

4.   *This woman has a sacred sense of concern for others.*

Because of the nearness and presence of Jesus in her life, she develops the God-given urge to share Him with others. She longs to reveal salvation's answers of love for living with all whom she meets. She has the mind of Christ in her thoughts. Imagine the joy of thinking His thoughts and revealing His love to others! She knows the beauty of the words in Acts 20:24, "But life is worth nothing unless

I use it for doing the work assigned me by the Lord Jesus—the work of telling others [in her home, her neighborhood, her business, and even her P.T.A.] the Good News about God's mighty kindness and love."

5. *This woman has a fragrant sense of spiritual power.*

She does not fear people—individually or in groups. She knows the Holy Spirit's power is at work within her. She carries out her duties with a delightful disposition, but she is quietly dynamic with power. Talk about a beauty—she's one! Can you see her? Do you know someone like her?

We can all be radiantly beautiful if we care to try. When Christ lives within us, we have these foregoing five senses at our beck and call. We don't have to live with passive, colorless personalities. We can accept God's forgiveness and claim His benefits. We can begin to really relate to people. We can live as we've never lived before. Our personalities can be enhanced beyond our fondest hopes. (God is quite a specialist in this department!)

When a woman really trusts Christ and believes what God has to say about her "oneness" with Him, her old ways can drop off like a rotten garment. Every faculty of her being can be energized anew by the Holy Spirit.

Paul really described what we could be like with the Holy Spirit's power working in our lives when he wrote, "But when the Holy Spirit controls our lives, He will produce this kind of fruit in us: love, joy, peace, patience, kindness, faithfulness, gentleness, and self-control. ... If we are living now by the Holy Spirit's power, let us follow the Holy Spirit's leading in every part of our lives. Then we won't need to look for honors and popularity which lead to jealousy and hard feelings" (Galatians 5:22,23,25,26).

The beautiful woman, whose life shows the fruit of the Spirit, exhibits some other practical qualities as well.

They are the qualities that make her personality real and down to earth.

1. *This woman has the fragrance of humor.*

She might not have been born with a great sense of humor, but she trains her mind to look at her life's happenings in good humor. She keeps her perspective. When she is a young wife and mother, she can smile (and even cope) during dinner's chaotic routine with little children. She is able to project a picture of herself in her mind's eye of a few years later when she will have no small children to spill their milk or ask her to cut up their meat. She can see herself in the years to come when the children have gone, and she is not afraid. She will warm herself by memories' fire and will recall a thousand dinners—by their fun giggling, by the outright laughter they enjoyed, and by their special private family jokes.

She will not take her life too seriously but will continually train herself to find the humor in it.

Her good sense of humor has helped her to take the three steps to real living which Peter talks about in 2 Peter 1:6-8. (1) "Learn to put aside your own desires so that you will become patient and godly, gladly letting God have his way with you. This will make possible the next step, which is for you to (2) enjoy other people and to like them, and finally you will (3) grow to love them deeply. The more you go on in this way, the more you will grow strong spiritually and become fruitful and useful to our Lord Jesus Christ."

2. *This woman has the fragrance of friendship.*

"A cheerful heart does good like medicine, but a broken spirit makes one sick" (Proverbs 17:22).

"Some women just make me sick," you've heard people say, and I'm sure it's because the women they refer to do not know or practice the art of *being* friendly. The woman who is friendly greets you with a warm smile whether she knows you or not!

She recognizes the tremendous therapeutic value of a smile in her home, to her husband and to her children. (Most husbands need a "buffer zone" between their work and their home. Some stop at a bar for a few drinks. Others drive home—*very slowly*.) The beautiful woman prepares herself to welcome others into her home. She greets everyone, including husband, children and neighbors in friendliness. Her spirit of friendship is motivated by the principle of Galatians 6:10: "Whenever we can we should always be kind to everyone, and especially to our Christian brothers."

3. *This woman has the fragrance of organization.*

She does not have this fanatic *thing* about cleanliness and being neat and tidy always. She does not drive anyone up a wall over a speck of dirt, but *she is neat*. Her house, according to the present rate of speed of their family life, has a semblance of order. She is not a slave chained to the mop, pail, and scrub brush, but her house is no cluttered, dirty, pigpen either. She's sure God does not want her to live in an unorganized mess of a house. (Nor is she a grooming disaster.)

The beautiful woman concentrates on her corner of the world and, while there, does her very best, as the following Scripture exhorts: "Let everyone be sure that he [or she] is doing his [or her] very best, for then he [or she] will have the personal satisfaction of work well done, and won't need to compare himself [or herself] with someone else" (Galatians 6:4).

4. *This woman has the fragrance of hospitality.*

She opens her home to others even when her couch is rather threadbare, the walls need paint, and she doesn't have enough dishes or chairs. She shares her dinner table, without apologies, and can be gracious even if it's only "hamburger night." She makes you feel that you have added the special magic ingredient to an evening just by being there. She never says, "Can I get you something?" She says, "Let's see, I have the hot water going—which will it be, coffee or tea?"

If you drop in on her unexpectedly, you take her (and her house) as is, and instantly she puts you at ease. She may say, "Good grief, I look awful, but come in; pardon the mess. How good to see you!" No apologies follow after that, and her hospitality remains a warm memory for a long time to come.

The fragrance of hospitality is enhanced by her concern involving the social graces. Etiquette is no dirty, nine-letter word to her. She practices and teaches manners as routinely as she practices and teaches Biblical truths. She knows "etiquette" is just another name for being kind to one another. (Many Christian families have forgotten that being kind to each other happens to be one of the secondary themes running the length of the New Testament.) When it's possible she privately seeks for her husband's cooperation in this venture. (Nothing teaches children to chew food with their mouths closed quite like a mother and father who chew food with their mouths closed!)

She does many things in the spirit of hospitality, but we rarely find out about them for she has heeded Jesus' admonition, "Take care! Don't do your good deeds publicly, to be admired, for then you will lose the reward from your Father in heaven. But when you do a kindness to someone, do it secretly—don't tell your left hand what your right hand is doing" (Matthew 6:1,3).

This practice of doing good in secret adds the clearest of twinkles to her already sparkling eyes!

5. *This woman has the fragrance of wonder.*

Nothing is too small or insignificant to catch her attention. She is interested in everything. She is beautiful when she teaches her children the sense of wonder by pointing out the little brown bug on the ground, the sleeping kitty, and the orange sunset. She works at keeping their natural wonder alive. She, herself, is so filled with wonder that she becomes an interesting, colorful person. She smiles and talks with her eyes, and her face lights up over the wonder of little things. She is a joy to see.

6.   *This woman has the fragrance of honesty.*

She does not lie—even about little things. If she is busy and does not want to answer her phone, she does not say to her children, "Tell them Mommie is not home." She says, "Tell them Mommie is busy and will call them back later." She teaches them honesty in the best of ways . . . by example.

Shortly after my friend Clare became a Christian, she was deeply convicted about a note she'd sent to school for her children's absences. She had claimed illness for their absence when actually they had gone on a short vacation.

She told me that after the Lord dealt with her conscience about it, leveling her pride a bit, she wrote a letter to the principal saying she'd lied and explaining that since she was now a Christian she wanted to right the wrong.

The principal read it as Clare stood there (another leveling moment) and then thoughtfully said, "In all the years I've been at this job, I've read thousands of excuse notes. Hundreds of them have been outright lies. This is the *very first* letter of confession I've ever received."

A beautiful woman doesn't lie about her age. She doesn't even have to hide how old she is. She's learned that all she really has to call her own is the moment she is living right now. She takes the years as they come. To her, each new year is just that . . . a new year, a new year of opportunity and possibility. She has accepted the fact that she is not one minute older or younger than God wants her to be! Because she doesn't lie about her age, God seems to age her gracefully.

Most Christian women rarely face the fact that they can and do lie. Not this beautiful woman who wrote:

> "Oh, yes, by the way, Joyce, just last week I discovered a terrible thing I do—I tell little lies! Oh, how shocking the hard faced truth of that was! Imagine after all these years of doing it and defending it [we usually justify the lie because our motives are good] I now see it as a sin— through God's eyes. I almost jumped out of my car seat when I saw and realized this. So, I confessed my lies, and I'm so happy. I've actually consistently begun telling the truth. In fact, I've had one whole week where I didn't tell one single lie. What a victory! It feels great!" (I know the feeling, Praise God!)

7.   *This woman has the fragrance of learning.*

She is not afraid to develop new skills. She tries to do something creative at least once a day—even if it's only adding a dash of paprika and parsley to her potatoes. She reads a wide range of books. She takes instruction, from a Bible study course to needlepoint classes or listens to tapes. She is enthusiastically dedicated to increasing her learning powers and her willingness to tackle a new project is gorgeous!

8.   *This woman has the fragrance of balanced priorities.*

The beautiful woman is one who has asked God about the goals and priorities of her life, and He has opened several new doors. First, she found she is a person—a woman—she is somebody! Then, she discovered, by much soul searching and praying, God's highly original list of what's-up-first for her life. The truly lovely woman does not want to be a carbon copy of even the most beautiful woman, but wants to be what God wants *her* to be. Some women can't handle marriage, child raising, and a job simultaneously. Others manage the whole bit with astonishing perfection. God deals individually with each of us, and what He may do in your life, He may not do in mine. If a woman keeps her check-list of priorities handy, she will be fragrant with the originality God has planned for her.

9.   *This woman has the fragrance of appreciation.*

She knows that in life the essence of appreciation is like butter and jam on dry toast: it makes it go down much easier. She has sincere thankfulness running through her veins. It is not the phony or gushy put-on type but a real appropriate sense of appreciation. She has days when she does not feel thankful (especially for an illness or at the death of a loved one), but she understands the nature of a God-allowed crisis. She knows God uses crises to develop and mature character. She does not hang on to her resentment of problems because she understands their work in her life. Whether she sees the results of being thankful or not, she knows God can be trusted.

She is not only obediently thankful, but also scatters seeds of genuine praise to everyone around her. Long after they have left a gathering, she says to her husband, "Oh, Hon, you said a beautiful thing tonight about so-and-so. Thank you for being you."

In the quiet of her daughter's bedroom, she says, "Sweetie, when I saw you tonight, standing beside those other kids, my heart just swelled with pride because God gave you to me!"

When someone compliments her, she responds with *"Thank you*—you've just made me feel so special."

She uses words to encourage and praise others, and the sound of her voice is the best sound in the world!

These nine fragrances are only a few of the truly beautiful woman's characteristics, but I pray you've caught the aroma and you're measuring and evaluating the fragrances of your own life.

The rain is still coming down, and I must close this book and lay aside my pen.

Just as I was writing I looked out our window and saw our pitiful rose garden. The rose bushes, poor darlings, are almost flooded out and their feelings are hurt because their stems have been severely pruned. They are not things of beauty at this moment. Not only are they pruned way back, but soon they will suffer the indignation of having their roots mulched. They will be sure the end is near. But it will get worse before it gets better because after their leaves start budding, they will have to be sprayed for aphids. Then the rose bushes will just know they'll never survive. But in a few short weeks, after they've been fed some special rose food, they will begin to have their first buds of bloom. These beauties will burst forth into full blossom in a glorious color that can only be described as "Shouting Pink." Since they are the Floribunda variety, they will grow in profusion. Rain or sun will not deter their efforts, and the fragrance—my, the fragrance—will just astound family and friends again this year.

The woman who has asked Christ into her life has the same fantastic potential for beauty as those rose bushes. She may not understand (or look forward to) the losses of the pruning season, but she knows pruning means growth, not death.

When her roots are disturbed, the change does not threaten to destroy or panic her. She looks to God for her strength. She feeds daily and regularly on His Word, and her roots grow deep into the soil of His love.

When the stinging spray of disappointment washes over her soul, she knows the suffering is only temporary. She hangs onto her faith and is a little surprised because she feels growth through it all.

When the rain beats down on her, she accepts it as God's way of washing off the diseases of fear, worry, insecurity, anger, and bitterness. She holds her head high and thinks the thoughts of God.

She prepares her heart for blooming with a running conversation with God, and she is kept enthusiastic by His words.

She blossoms into the fragrant, colorful flower God has uniquely designed her to be.

She knows that no matter how a woman fixes her face or her hair or takes care of her outer looks, if she does not have Christ, she will have no real beauty. She will be like a flower with no perfume, no fragrance, no essence to remember.

The beautiful woman of God knows exactly who made her. She is an original design, and she is loved by her Maker.

Saint Augustine, in the Tenth Book of Confessions, wrote:

> I asked the earth and it answered,
> "I am not He,"
> and whatsoever are in it
> confessed the same.
>
> I asked the sea and the depths
> and the living, creeping things,
> and they answered,
> "We are not thy God.
> Seek above us."
>
> I asked the moving air,
> the heavens, sun, moon and stars.
> "Nor, (say they) are we the God
> whom thou seekest."

And I replied unto all things
which encompass the door of my flesh,

"Ye have told me of my God,
that ye are not He;
Tell me something of Him!"
and they cried out with a loud voice,

"He made us ... we are not God,
But He made us!"

Just think of that—*He made us!* Ruth Harms Calkin wrote
in her poem, *Something Beautiful*:

Here I am, dear God
Your child
A member of Your Family
Asking You
To make something beautiful
Of my life.
Yet, even as I ask
I am convinced
That the one beautiful thing
About a child of God
Is You, Jesus Christ.
So, dear Lord
As You saturate me with Yourself
My life will be beautiful.

The woman who understands the truth of who she
is and why she's loved is completely surrounded by a
fragrance. It is an unmistakable fragrance, swirling around
her in a fine, penetrating mist. It is the real, the God-given,
fragrance of beauty!

This woman is what every Christ-centered woman can
and should be ...

BEAUTIFUL, BEYOND WORDS!

Additional Scripture references for this chapter.

Honesty	Ephesians 4:15 TLB
Lying	1 Peter 3:10 TLB
Resisting temptation	1 Corinthians 10:13 TLB 1 Peter 1:14 TLB
Thankfulness	Proverbs 20:12 TLB 1 Thessalonians 5:18 TLB
Attitudes	Philippians 2:5-7 TLB Philippians 2:14-16 TLB
Obeying	1 Peter 2:13 TLB
Needing others	Genesis 2:23,24 TLB 1 Corinthians 11:11 TLB 1 Corinthians 12 TLB Hebrews 10:25 TLB
Living	Revelation 3:8 TLB

ABOUT THE AUTHOR

Joyce Landorf Heatherley is known nationwide as a uniquely gifted Christian communicator, able to convey Biblical principles with relevance, humor, compassion and gentle conviction—in a way that speaks to the needs of men and women from all backgrounds. A best-selling author of both fiction and non-fiction, her 22 books include: BALCONY PEOPLE, SILENT SEPTEMBER, MONDAY THROUGH SATURDAY, FRAGILE TIMES, IRREGULAR PEOPLE, HE BEGAN WITH EVE, CHANGEPOINTS, UNWORLD PEOPLE, MOURNING SONG, JOSEPH, I CAME TO LOVE YOU LATE, FRAGRANCE OF BEAUTY, and THE INHERITANCE.

Joyce Landorf Heatherley is also an immensely popular speaker and conference leader. Recordings of her more popular talks, including: BALCONY PEOPLE, IRREGULAR PEOPLE, UNWORLD PEOPLE and THE INHERITANCE are available on audio cassette, as are video tapes of CHANGEPOINTS, IRREGULAR PEOPLE, and UNWORLD PEOPLE. Her HIS STUBBORN LOVE film series, based on her nationally acclaimed seminars of the same name, was the recipient of the 1981 President's Award from the Christian Film Distributors Association.

Any speaking engagement requests or inquiries concerning Joyce Landorf Heatherley books, tapes, and films may be directed to 1-800-777-7949.